Tequila is
to Kill Ya

Tequila is to Kill Ya

Remy O'Brien

To order additional copies of this book, contact:
Xlibris Corporation
1-888-795-4274
www.Xlibris.com
Orders@Xlibris.com
55677

Chapter 1

Carson moaned as bright sunlight sneaked through the crack of the blinds and glared onto her face. She smacked her tongue against the pasty roof of her mouth, the taste unbearable. Her left eye peered at the clock and quickly closed again when she saw it wasn't in the right spot. Cautiously, she opened both eyes and stared up at the ceiling, then turned her head to the left and cringed at the sleeping nightmare beside her.

"Damn, damn, damn," she muttered to herself. She really needed to quit drinking.

Pulling up the sheet, she looked at herself and thanked an angel above. Her pants were still on. But her shirt and bra were missing. She inched to the edge of the bed and peered underneath, catching a glimpse of her bra and a piece of balled-up cloth. She knew it was her shirt.

Scooting closer to the edge, she stretched out her hand until her fingers reached the bra and she was able to pull it in. With that accomplished, she stretched once again, this time going for the shirt. The tips of her fingers brushed across the fabric. She just needed to move a little closer, a little more of a stretch . . .

"Ugh," she grunted as her body fell from the bed and hit the hardwood floor. Carson lay there a minute, afraid she'd awaken her nightmare. Unable to stand the cold floor against her chest, with her shirt in hand, she stood up and stared into smirking green eyes.

"Leaving so soon?" He tucked his hands behind his head as he lay back on the bed.

Carson turned her back, clipped on her bra, and jammed her arms into her dirty, strawberry-stained work shirt. Half-finished buttoning her top, she almost made it past the bed before his hand snaked out and grabbed her wrist.

"Let go," she demanded.

"Don't you want to finish what you started last night?" He placed her hand on his hard-on.

She yanked free of his grasp, thoroughly revolted, bile rising in her throat. "I don't think so."

"What, change of heart so early in the morning?"

"No. Just sober enough to realize what a mistake I almost made."

"That's not what you said last night." He reached for her.

She jumped back. "Jack, I'm sorry. I should never have come here."

"The only thing you should be sorry about is denying both of us what we want. We're good together, and you know it."

"We have no future."

"You're never going to forgive me for that one stupid night, are you?"

Had it been just one night? She'd never know, but there was more than his infidelity. Her eyes scanned the room. The walls were cluttered with all types of sports memorabilia. Even his bed sheets displayed his favorite football team. She felt like she was in a twelve-year-old boy's room, not a thirty-year-old man's.

"There's more to it than that. We aren't right for each other. I knew that five years ago when we first started dating and a year ago when it was over."

"It doesn't have to be over." His eyes pleaded with her. "Or else you wouldn't keep coming back for more."

Carson headed toward the door. He was right behind her. She opened it, and he slammed it closed.

"Come on, Carson," he said, his breath warm on her ear. "You know you still love me."

The feel of his muscled chest against her back stirred nothing in her. It was just like she thought. It was the alcohol. "There's nothing between us anymore. I'm sorry." And she truly was.

"You can't keep waltzing in here anytime you feel like it. Drunk or not."

"Don't worry. I won't be coming back. Good-bye, Jack."

"Yeah, right. Good-bye."

She opened the door a second time.

"Oh, and, Carson, just one more thing. Happy birthday," he sneered. "How does it feel to be thirty, alone, and in a dead-end job?"

She slammed the door behind her and walked away, not once looking back.

She sat in her '93 hunter green corvette and felt the tears burn the backs of her eyes. She stared at herself in the rearview mirror. "You promised you wouldn't do this, Carson," she berated herself. "So what if you just turned thirty? So what if you haven't found Mr. Perfect? So what if you're still just a bartender with a college degree?"

Her eyes were puffy and bloodshot from too much drinking. She patted the skin under her chin—an exercise she started in high school to keep the skin from sagging and creating a double chin. The clock read nine forty-five. Great, she had fifteen minutes to get to work. There was no way she'd be able to get home and shower in time. At least she'd have a clean uniform; she always kept one in her car.

She opened up the glove compartment and pulled out her backup deodorant. Quickly, she glided the stick under her left underarm four times and then did the same with her right one. Sniffing under each armpit and still not satisfied with the results, she grabbed her bottle of Cool Water perfume and sprayed it under her arms, down her breasts, behind both ears.

Carson sped down the highway, hoping her luck would hold and she wouldn't get pulled over. She'd definitely lose her insurance then. "Think positive," she said to herself in the rearview mirror. "This is your day, you're thirty." Looking back at the road, she noticed a blue sedan beside her. The man was yelling and pointing for her to pull over. Half-afraid he was some type of the lunatic, she sped up until she looked back at the car and saw the red flashing bubble light on the dashboard.

"Shit, shit, shit," she screamed as she banged on the steering wheel. She pulled over.

She rolled her window down and waited for him to reach the car. "Yes, sir." She smiled sweetly, she hoped.

"Do you realize how fast you were going?" he asked, his voice was clipped.

Decisions, should she admit that she did or pretend ignorance? She looked at her watch and wondered which one would get her to work quicker. She opted for neutral. "I'm sorry, er . . . ," she paused, not sure how to address him since he wasn't wearing a uniform. "I'm going to be late for work."

"Oh, so because you can't get up early enough to get to work, you need to endanger others' lives, including my own."

Carson could feel her plastered smile slipping. He didn't need to be so nasty, and frankly, she didn't need it this morning. "Excuse me, sir, but you don't need to talk to me like that." She willed the tears to stay hidden.

"How about I don't talk? How about I take you to the police station and charge you with reckless endangerment?"

"Wh-what?" She felt the remains of last night's alcohol rise up her throat.

"Better yet." He sniffed. "Maybe I need to give you a sobriety test. One I'm sure you'd fail."

"I . . . I'm not drunk, Officer. I swear it." This time she was unable to stop a tear from falling.

"Let me see your driver's license and registration."

She pulled her license from her back pocket then fumbled around her glove compartment for a few minutes until she found the registration. Before she could relinquish them, he ripped them out of her hand.

"You're welcome," she mumbled under her breath.

"What was that?"

"Nothing, Officer." She wiped the tears from her face. Why couldn't she be like those women who just smiled and played dumb? She and cops just didn't mesh. She never got off with a warning or "have a nice day." He appeared back at the window with a ticket in hand. "Here you go, Ms. O'Hara. Slow it down."

"Thanks." She grabbed the citation, not even looking at it; she put the car in gear. She glared at him, hoping he'd take the hint and step away.

"Happy birthday, Ms. O'Hara." He walked off.

Carson was still fuming when she drove into the lot and whipped her corvette into a parking spot.

"Two minutes to spare. Good job, Carson," she congratulated herself. She looked at the ticket she'd thrown on the passenger seat. Might as well see how much this one cost. She picked it up then smiled broadly.

He'd given her a warning. "Thank you, God." She clasped her hands together. This just might be a good day after all.

She grabbed her backup uniform and ran to the front of the restaurant.

Kansas, the name of the restaurant she worked in, was a casual dining steak house. It was a beautiful building; the outside was light brown brick with a stack stone entryway. The double doors were beveled glass; the outer part made with a dark cherry wood, the same color of the booths that were inside. In gold letters on the glass were the names of the general manager and the kitchen manager.

Carson rolled her eyes as she did every time she walked through the doors and read, Peter Boston, General Manager.

She couldn't stand the little weasel, and she knew he didn't care too much for her either, but she was his number one bartender. She'd been there longer than he had, and most of the regulars came to see her. Especially on Friday night happy hours, their busiest night.

Carson pulled open the doors, plastered her "I love my job" smile on her lips, and hoped it got her through the rest of the day. She headed through the lobby past the open kitchen—there was no wall blocking the guests from watching the food preparation, and it was part of the charm—over to the computer and punched in number 79, her employee number, the same one she had punched in for the past five years. "Don't think about it. You'll leave this place one day." She sighed to herself.

She made her morning rounds. A quick hello to the dishwasher, a wave to the prep guy, a "what's up?" to Cindy the salad girl and a quick "how are the kids?" A little flirting with the line guys, whom she depended upon to put her order together quickly; then she hugged, winked, and gossiped with Tootsie, the dessert maker, for a bit. After that, she waltzed back into the office to check on the unit accountant who was one of her best friends.

"Hey, sweetie," Carson called out as she opened the door.

"Carson," Jamie replied in that thick Tulsa accent that Carson adored. Jessie took one look at Carson and said, "You look like shit—*shit* pronounced *shee-it*."

"Why, thank you, Jessie. It's good to see you this morning too."

"Don't give me that. You know it too. That's why you came in here, bearing me gifts." She took a sip of the coffee Carson brought her. "You need little ol' Jessie's help fixing it." She grabbed her purse from under her worktable and got up. "Come on, let's go."

They headed to the other end of the restaurant and entered the bathroom. Jessie opened her purse and pulled out her Cinderella kit. She made Carson lean against the sink and proceeded to work her magic.

"So," Jessie began, "judging by the looks of it, I'd say after you got off work, you noticed it was nearing midnight, yah freaked out about turning the big three-oh, went down to Baileys, had one too many Sambucas, and?" She fixed Carson with her gaze.

"And what?" Carson replied, unable to look her in the eye.

"Fine, you don't have to tell me. But I know you went over to Jack's house, and you probably hate yourself right now. Just—"

"Jessie, I don't—"

Jessie held up both hands. "All I want to say is that you are a beautiful, caring person, and there is someone out there for you. Don't settle because you're afraid he's all there is."

Carson felt tears once again.

"Oh, sweetie, don't beat yourself up too much. It's your birthday. Enjoy it."

Carson eyed her friend. She was one of three people who knew her so well. Abby, who just moved to New Orleans to be with her boyfriend, and Emily, who was off in Hawaii chasing the perfect wave.

Carson sighed and shook her head. "You know me too well, I can't get anything past you. Right down to what I drank. You amaze me."

"I should let you think I'm that good. The truth is you smell like a brewery with a hint of licorice. That's how I guessed the Sambuca." They both laughed.

After a few more touch-ups, Jessie was done. "Voila, once again the lovely Ms. Carson is a beauty."

"Thanks, Jessie, you're a doll." She took a quick peek to check the transformation—wow. Jessie was good. It was just the lift she needed to get her through this horrid day.

Jessie headed back toward the kitchen while Carson strode straight to the bar.

She eyed the half-moon-shaped bar with its twenty barstools and granite top, hoping she'd make it through the next six hours without tossing her cookies. At least, it was the lunch shift. Thankfully, she'd served more food than booze. The thought of alcohol made her stomach churn. "Stop dawdling and get to work," she berated herself.

Carson headed back to the kitchen, retrieved three large buckets, filled them with ice, and then lugged them up to the bar, making four trips. Well, at least, she wouldn't feel guilty about missing the gym today. She eyed the half-empty beer cooler and then cursed herself for having been too lazy last night to refill it. Back to the kitchen she went, maneuvered a few different six-packs into the cases, and hauled them back up front. The next ten minutes were busied with cutting different fruits, making strawberry mix and piña colada mix, and squeezing three containers each of fresh orange juice and grapefruit.

She leaned back against the bar, turned on the two TVs that hung on the wall, and flipped them to ESPN to numb her mind until her first guest arrived.

*   *   *

Chapter 2

Carson started feeling the effects of last night's escapades at around two o'clock in the afternoon, right after the lunch rush. She couldn't wait to leave this place, head home, and crash. *Forget going out tonight,* she thought. She'd spend her thirtieth birthday alone. She needed the peace and quiet.

"Hey, doll, the usual." The crazy old coot hoisted his rear onto the redwood barstool.

"Hey, Henry." She popped open the Miller Lite and placed it in front of him.

"Henry, what are you doing here so early?" She looked into his craggy old face. He was one of her favorite regulars. Although she wasn't sure how true they were, she loved listening to his lively stories

"Ah. The missus just wouldn't get off my back this morning. So I'm actually here late. If I were just twenty years younger and—"

"I was twenty years older," she finished for him. He used that line on her at least once a week.

Another customer sat at the bar, drawing her attention.

"Hi, Sharon," Carson said, "what are you drinking today?" Carson knew what Sharon drank, it was the same every day, but Sharon demanded that Carson ask every time. Carson, not one to upset her regulars, did what made them happy.

"I'll have a CC and water with a twist of lemon."

"Okay. Are you going to have something to eat today?"

"Maybe later."

Carson made the drink and settled it in front of Sharon.

"Carson." Henry waved her down.

"Another one, Henry?"

"Nah, I don't need any more of that woman's blistering today." Henry reached into his back pocket for his wallet. "How much do I owe you?"

"Well, Henry, you're too early for happy hour; so it's going to cost you three bucks."

He pulled a ten out of his pocket and passed it to her. "Keep it."

She almost fainted. The most he ever left her was fifty cents.

"Happy birthday, Carson."

"Thanks, Henry, and good luck with Betsy." Pleased that he had remembered her birthday, Carson smiled. Then again, she shouldn't be that surprised. The other bartenders had been razzing her all week about hitting thirty.

"It's nothing, but you better go out and enjoy yourself tonight." Henry climbed off the barstool and slowly made his way out the front door. He turned back, offered her one more wave, and disappeared.

"Bye, Henry, see you next week," Carson yelled out. That was one of the great perks of her job, she had the weekends off. And that was virtually unheard-of in the restaurant business.

Carson scanned the length of the bar. Only Sharon remained. Not that Carson didn't like Sharon, but talking to her was depressing. Nothing ever seemed right in Sharon's life, which reminded Carson of her own problems.

Oh well. She was almost done. Only thirty minutes more. Then she could go home and dream this day away. She waltzed down to converse with Sharon.

"Hey, Sharon, so how's your day going."

Sharon sucked down the rest of her drink. "I lost my job today."

"Oh, Sharon. I'm so sorry. Here, let me make you another drink." She quickly mixed her drink and placed it in front of Sharon. "This one's on me."

"Thanks, Car. You're sweet. I think I'll be . . ."

Carson's eyes strayed to the clock. "I'm sure it will work out." Carson turned back to Sharon.

"I'll just collect unemployment."

"Yeah. Good." Carson tried to keep eye contact and stay focused. Her eyes went to the clock once again. Fifteen more minutes.

Carson's mind reeled. She had hoped her replacement would come in early. Then she remembered who it was.

"Fat chance," she spoke loud.

"What?" Sharon asked.

"I said that's too bad." Carson focused her full attention on Sharon.

Before Sharon could restart her story, Carson heard her name being called and turned toward the five guys that had walked through the front door. Her "Friday happy hour" boys, she called them. They worked across the highway at the new office building. They'd taken a liking to her as well as to the half-price beer, and no Friday happy hour went by without them. But she'd have to disappoint them today since she wasn't staying.

"Hey, guys." She popped open five beers and plopped them on the bar in front of them.

She turned to the register and rang up five separate checks. God forbid if someone got stuck paying an extra buck and fifty for somebody else's beer. She wrote their names on their checks. There were two Kevins, Steve, Charlie, and Puck.

She sat her butt up on the edge of the beer cooler, leaned her elbow on the bar top, and started talking to her new arrivals.

They'd only been talking for a minute when a whirlwind busted through the bar, and its name was Theresa.

"Hey, Carson. I made it. I was so afraid I'd be late, and I know you want to leave early. Being that it's your birthday and all."

"Birthday?" This was from Kevin number one. "You didn't tell us it was your birthday. You have to stay and let us buy you a birthday drink."

"Yeah," the rest of them piped in.

"Guys, I don't know."

"Come on. One little drink. Please."

"I don't . . ."

"By the looks of it, you could use a little hair of the dog."

Carson ran her hand through her hair. "Gee. Thanks, Puck."

"I'm not implying anything. You just have that look in your eye. The same one I have every Saturday morning."

"Just one beer, Carson," all five piped in again.

"Oh, all right, one drink." No one had to twist her arm too hard when it came to free drinks. Who knew when she'd get the offer *again*.

"I'll be back in a few minutes."

She turned in her bank—every shift the restaurant gave the bartenders a bank of three hundred dollars. Everything looked good. Knowing she had to follow management's rules, she hurried out to her car to change her clothes and then re-entered the restaurant as a guest.

The fact that she didn't have to see this place for the next two days made her feel better than she had an hour ago. She'd have one drink, head home, and veg out in front of the TV, unless Mr. Perfect, whomever that might be, called her and tempted her to leave her apartment.

Her smile faded as she turned the corner of the building and saw the long-legged, too sexy of a cop from this morning leaning against her car.

Definitely not Mr. Perfect. Shit, shit, shit. Why was he here? Did he have a change of heart? Was he going to give her a ticket? Her nausea returned.

She considered turning around and heading back in the restaurant, but she knew the minute he spotted her because he waved. Dread filled her as she slowly made her way to her car.

Under normal circumstance, she'd enjoy having a man like that waiting for her. But this one was a cop, and she and cops were like oil and water. *It's funny*, she thought. She'd studied prelaw in college and had been a few days away from starting training at the police academy until her dreams were shattered. She pushed the ugly memories away. She didn't look good in blue anyway, and the bartender business wasn't so bad.

Yeah, right.

"Ms. O'Hara," he greeted her when she reached the car.

"Officer." She nodded.

"Hunter."

"Officer Hunter."

"It's detective. But you can call me by my first name, Hunter." He pulled off his glasses.

The brilliant aquamarine of his eyes startled her.

She'd never seen eyes that color before. Once again, she found herself wishing he wasn't a cop, but it really didn't matter. Men like him either married the prettiest girl they could find or slept around until their looks faded then settled for what they could.

"You have a beautiful car. It's a '93, isn't it?"

"Yes, Offi—Hunter, the anniversary addition. Might be a collector's item one day." No need to tell him it was used and that she'd gotten it for a steal.

"You know you should really treat a car like this a little nicer," he said, peering inside at the litter-strewn seats.

"Just like a man to criticize a woman's car." She'd never admit that he was right. She'd promised herself time and again that she'd keep her vehicle spotless, but usually, one thing led to another. She was either running late to work and didn't have time to eat, so she'd scarf something down and then leave the wrappings in the car. Or she'd pick her dry-cleaning up on the way to work, leaving the plastic covering, safety pins, and hangers on the floor. Maybe this time she'd make good on her promise. There she went again, thinking about changing her ways because some gorgeous man made a comment.

"Detective, is there something you wanted?"

"Rough night?"

"Well, Detective. First, you insult the way I keep my car, and then you comment on how I look. If you're trying to score points, you're not doing a very good job. So if you're through insulting me, I'd like to go home now." She hoped her tone sounded cool enough. She didn't want him to know how his comments hurt her. And why she should be hurt? Because he was a gorgeous man and a little part of her would like to know him better. She really needed some sleep; her thoughts were getting too stupid. She looked up at him. "Please move so I can get into my car."

"We need to talk." He moved away from the door handle.

Great, she thought. *What did I do this time?*

"Let me guess, you decided not to be nice to me on my birthday and give me a ticket after all." She felt tears prick the back of her eyes, but she willed them away. There was no way she'd cry in front of this man, again.

"Ms. O'Hara, look—" He grabbed her hand before she could insert her key. She looked down, expecting to see smoke rising from his electrifying touch. Then she wondered if he felt it too because within seconds, he broke contact.

"I need you to come down to the station with me," he said.

"Why?" She swallowed over a knot in her throat. "Since when does a speeding violation demand someone to go down to the station?" She wondered if there was some type of jail time for having too many tickets in a year. Damn that lead foot of hers.

"You can follow me in your car." He walked away without answering.

She sucked in the cold air as she watched him walk to his car; then she got into hers and sat numbly behind the wheel. Her hands shook so hard she could barely get the key in the ignition. After a minute, she succeeded in starting the car. This couldn't be happening to her. Turning thirty was supposed to be the turnaround of her life, her starting-over point. No more stupid mistakes. She had promised herself that she'd slow down on the drinking, be more selective in the guys she dated, and maybe even look for a different career.

The drive to the station seemed to take forever. She could honestly say that was the slowest she'd driven her car since she bought it.

She'd never been inside a police station before. Hunter led her through the white metal doors, down a thin hallway, and went up to a window.

"Hello, Delores," he said to the woman behind the glass, barely slowing his pace.

"Hello, Hunter." Delores pressed her face against the glass with a look that said she longed for him to look back.

If Carson hadn't been so scared, she might have laughed. He probably slept with the woman once, she thought. And she'd been chasing him ever since. Carson knew the type. She shook away the thought.

She heard a buzzing sound, and then Hunter pushed open another door. She hadn't known what to expect; but it wasn't secret doors, pristine white walls, and a small group of officers.

"Boy, TV sure had it wrong," Carson whispered.

"What?" Hunter leaned into her.

"Nothing." She pulled back.

Hunter escorted her to a desk, waved her into a seat, then went around to the other side and sat behind the desk.

"Before we start, can I get you something to drink?" he asked.

"How about a shot of tequila?" By the way his head jerked up, she knew she'd said something wrong.

"I . . . I was only kidding," she stammered.

"Do you drink shots of tequila often?"

"Huh? What? No." In fact, she hated tequila. Hoping to appease him, she added. "That stuff will kill you."

"And what do you know about people dying from tequila?" his voice clipped. "Maybe you and some of your friends were out drinking tequila by the lake last night."

She didn't know what was going on, but his tone caused her heart to race. She felt a thin line of sweat trickle down her breast.

"What makes you think I was drinking last night?" She shifted her gaze downward, unable to lie to someone's face.

"For one, I pulled you over this morning, remember? I smelled hints of alcohol. And second, you're a terrible liar, Ms. O'Hara."

Ignoring his second comment, she said, "Look, Officer, I don't know what this is about; but I believe it's too late to give me a DWI. So if you don't mind, I'll be going home now." She started to get up.

"Ms. O'Hara. What were you drinking last night?"

She bit her lower lip. "Okay, I did have a couple of beers. That's it. I swear it. I celebrated my birthday a little early. That's all."

"With whom," he shot back.

"Some friends from work," she replied.

"What time?"

"Well, uh—"

"What time, Ms. O'Hara?"

Carson shook. "Just let me think a minute." She shut up a second before going on. "I got off work around twelve thirty. It takes about twenty minutes to get to Baileys. So I'd say around one-ish or so." She assumed she answered correctly because he stopped looking so serious, and his shoulders relaxed.

She let out a breath she didn't know she'd been holding. "Could you tell me what this is all about?" she asked.

"We found a dead woman late last night."

"What does a dead woman have to do with me?"

"I'm not sure. The only thing we found on her was an address. We traced it back to you."

"That doesn't make any sense. Why would a dead woman have my address?"

"That's what I was hoping you'd be able to tell us."

She crinkled her eyes. "It had to be a mistake." Then it suddenly dawned on her that this wasn't about her at all. The jerk had scared her for nothing. She turned on him.

"You asshole!" She stood up and placed her hands on his desk. She took grim satisfaction at the fact that her sudden outburst had him pull back in his chair.

"You made me believe I'd done something wrong. That I was getting arrested."

"I never said I was arresting you." He sat back in his chair. "Let me explain."

"Explain what? That you're a bully who likes to harass women. You probably got your kicks in high school by making girls cry." It felt good to see his face turn red.

"Did I hit a nerve, Detective Reeves?"

"Please sit down and be quiet," he warned.

"I will not sit down and shut up, you jerk. I'm out of here." She turned to leave and noticed the whole office was quiet. All eyes were upon her. She didn't care, let them stare.

She reached the door, fought with it a few minutes before she remembered she had to be buzzed out. She looked back at Hunter.

"Ms. O'Hara. Please sit back down."

Knowing that her grand departure was being foiled, she crossed her arms over her chest then mouthed, "Open the door."

All eyes that had been turned to her now turned to Hunter. "I'm warning you, Ms. O'Hara. Sit down."

Eyes turned back to her.

She marched back to his desk. "Would you please let me out?" she said through gritted teeth.

"Not until you tell me if you know this girl!" He threw the photos of the dead woman on the desk in front of her.

She picked up the picture. "Why would I know . . . ? Oh my god, Em!" The photo fell from her hands. She felt her knees go weak and would have fallen if not for the guy at the next desk who sprung up and caught her.

Chapter 3

The young officer placed her in a seat and asked, "Are you all right?"

She looked up at the stranger, tears streaming down her face. "Tell me this is a bad dream."

"You know her then." Hunter soothingly confirmed.

Carson could barely see him through her haze of tears. She tried to speak, but the words were a choked sob.

"Come on." Hunter helped raise her out of the chair and took her to a gray, cold windowless interrogation room. He placed her in a wooden chair next to the table then disappeared.

Carson laid her head upon the scar-worn table and let the tears take over. "Why? Why? Why?" she screamed between sobs.

"Here. Drink this." Hunter had returned and placed a glass of water in her hands. She took the water but barely got a sip past the tears still in her throat.

"Take all the time you need," he coaxed as he handed her a box of tissue.

Carson grabbed a handful and, in an unladylike fashion, blew her nose. She wiped her eyes with the palms of her hands.

"Who is she?"

She hiccupped. "Her name's Em-Emily."

She hadn't used her full name in years. Em had started it by calling her Car, a name that had stuck with her through the years, and Carson had called her Em. She was the only one who did. Her bottom lip quivered at the memory.

"Drink some more water." Hunter pushed the glass in front of her.

Carson took another sip, but it didn't stop her from crying again. "I'm sorry," she wailed.

Hunter motioned for Carson to rise. "I'm going to take you home. I won't put you through this right now. But I'd like to meet with you tomorrow and get some information. Okay?"

A nod was all she could muster.

He escorted her out of the interrogation room. "Norton," he called to his new partner, "I need you to follow me to Ms. O'Hara's place."

In zombielike fashion, Carson walked beside Hunter. She was only vaguely aware of leaving the station with Hunter helping her into the passenger seat of her car.

Hunter drove down Highway 65, heading south to Franklin, Tennessee. She had to be dreaming. Em couldn't be dead. Oh god, when was the last time she talked to Emily? Why hadn't she called more often? Did Em know how much Carson loved her? "Em, I'm so sorry."

"What?" Hunter asked.

Carson jumped. She forgot all about Hunter. Keeping her gaze focused on the road, she answered.

"Her full name is Emily Johnson." Carson sucked in a big breath. "We've been best friends since we were twelve. We played on the same softball team together every summer until high school. We were both on the cheerleading squad. Em was way better than I ever could be." A slight smile curved Carson's lips as she stared out the window.

"I'm sorry for your loss. I know how it feels to lose someone you care for." He squeezed her hand and held it.

She thought how funny it seemed that barely an hour ago, his touch had ignited something deep inside her while this time, she just found comfort in the huge hand that smothered hers. She couldn't recall a time a man's touch gave her comfort. Hunter held her hand until they reached her apartment; then he released it to step out of the car.

After a second's hesitation, Carson followed his lead. She still felt numb. "I'll be right back," he told her. Then he walked over to his partner.

She watched him peer into the other guy's window and exchange a few words. Then he trotted back over to her and led her up the flight of stairs to her second-floor apartment. He unlocked the door and escorted her down the short hallway to the living room. Although the room still had some light from the setting sun, he turned on the table lamp.

"Now I know how you can afford that car of yours."

For the first time, she took a good look at her apartment. Her furniture was sparse; a love seat, a recliner, an end table with a lamp, a twenty-inch television, a little Aiwa radio, and a small oak table in the little dining room area was all that she possessed.

Carson collapsed onto the love seat and pulled her legs up, hugging her knees into her chest.

"Here." Hunter draped a blanket across Carson's shoulders. "You're shivering."

"Thank you." Carson pulled the blanket into her body.

"Would you like me to fix you something to eat before I go?" He went to the kitchen before Carson could answer.

"No wonder you're so little," he yelled out. "You actually call this stuff food." He returned to the living room and placed a plate of cheese and apples as well as a bottled water on the table next to the couch.

"Thank you." She tried to smile.

"Well, I better get going. I'd like to stop by tomorrow about noon, if that's all right?" He headed toward the door.

"Have her parents been contacted?" she called out. He let go of the doorknob and turned to her. "We didn't know who she was until you told us."

Fresh tears cascaded down her cheeks. Carson never saw him move from the door, but within seconds, she was in his arms.

"It's okay, let it out."

After she calmed down, she pulled away from him. "I'm sorry, I got you all wet." She rubbed at the damp spot on his shoulder.

"Don't worry, it comes with the territory." He looked into her eyes.

"I'm sure it does." She wiped the tears from her eyes.

"Are you going to be okay? Is there someone you want me to call?"

"Yes, but not for me. Em's parents still think she's in Hawaii. They need to know she's . . . d-dead." The new waves of tears wracked her body.

Hunter reached for her, but she put her hand up to stop him. "Please just go talk to Emily's parents." She gave him the number, walked him to the door, and locked it behind him.

She crawled into bed knowing she'd never sleep a wink.

*   *   *

No longer able to watch the clock's numbers flip, Carson decided to get out of bed. She went into the kitchen and made herself a pot of coffee.

The message light on her answering machine was blinking. She never had a chance to check it the night before.

Carson hit the Play button and listened as the digital voice said, "You have four new messages.

"First message received at nine a.m. 'Carson, honey, it's Mom. Happy birthday. Call us, love ya.'" *Beep.*

The digital voice again said, "Second message at ten a.m. 'Carson, it's your mother again still waiting for your call.'"

Carson listened to the third message that came at 4:00 p.m. "Hey, Carson, it's Jack. I'm really sorry about this morning. I'd like to take you out to dinner for your birthday. Please give me a call."

And the last message received at six p.m. was once again her mother. "I guess you still aren't home. Maybe you're out on a date. It's about time. I hope he's a nice, rich young man. Because now that you're thirty, your time is running out. You know by the time I was your age, I had your third brother—" Carson erased it midway through, having heard it a thousand times every birthday since she turned twenty-one.

She poured herself a cup of coffee when the phone rang again. Not up to dealing with her mother, she let the answering machine pick it up.

Hot coffee sloshed on her hand as she jerked at the sound of the voice on the other end.

"Carson, honey, it's Mrs. Johnson. Please call us, we have some news about Emily."

Carson put the coffee cup down on the counter and went into the bathroom. Hunter hadn't told them she knew, but why? She got into the shower and sank down to the floor, welcoming the pounding hot water as tears she thought she could no longer shed wracked her body.

* * *

Five days had passed since Carson lost her best friend. Carson hadn't seen or spoken to Hunter since that night. He had called while she was in the shower and left a message saying that he had all he needed and that he wouldn't have to cause her more grief. She felt foolish when she thought about how she had waited for him to call. He had been so sweet and comforting that night. She had actually believed he might have liked her a little bit.

Then she remembered he was a cop, and a handsome one at that, and figured she'd never hear from him again.

Carson almost yelped from the pinch that Jessie delivered to the back of her arm. Carson was about to pinch Jessie back when she heard Father John announce her name. Then she realized he must have said it before because everyone present turned to her. She took a deep breath and then stood.

As she made her way up the aisle to give the eulogy, she hoped no one noticed how clingy her black dress was. She had spent most of the morning stretching it. Though black was her favorite color in clothing, the only black dresses she had were strictly meant for the clubs. She hadn't had time to shop for a new one.

Her mom—who had shown up unexpectedly as soon as she heard about Emily—had offered her one of her dresses. But Carson refused to wear anything with rhinestones that had her looking like she belonged onstage at the *Grand Ole Opry* instead of a funeral.

Once she was at the pulpit, it took her a few minutes to find her voice. By the time she finished, there wasn't a dry eye in the church except for hers. She hadn't cried since the day after Emily's death and vowed she wouldn't again.

Mr. and Mrs. Johnson waited for her as she descended from the altar, embraced her while they whispered thank-you in her ear. She took her seat next to Jessie—who was balling her eyes out—and hugged her. "It'll be all right."

There was no burial. As per Em's request, she'd been cremated; and her parents were taking her ashes to California, where she was originally from, and giving her body back to the ocean.

Carson stood alone on the church steps, surveying the clusters of mourners until she found the Johnsons. To her amazement, they weren't alone. Hunter was with them. He was hotter than she remembered. Not that she could recall too much of the past five days. Just looking at him filled her stomach with butterflies. Suddenly, the flutters were replaced by a sinking feeling.

A vision of blue polyester pants, brown cowboy boots, and brown suede jacket with fringed sleeves, known as her mother, appeared next to Hunter.

She had tried to talk her mother into staying in Florida, but it hadn't worked. Now here she was, dogging Carson everywhere she went. She hadn't had a moment's peace since her arrival.

It took Carson three seconds to reach the group. She threw Mr. and Mrs. Johnson a "sorry you have to deal with my mom today" look. Mrs. Johnson just patted her hand in understanding. Not that her mother was a bad person. It's just she was her mom, and there was no other way to explain it.

"Carson, honey, you didn't tell me you had such a good-looking, charming, as well as single friend," her mother cooed as she patted her maroon-colored hair.

Carson closed her eyes. Blast her mother and her infernal matchmaking.

Instead, it was Hunter's voice that chimed in, "Hello, Carson. It's good to see you again."

She longed to echo the same sentiment, but she caught the Cheshire-cat grin on her mom's face and decided not to fuel the fire. If her mom had even an inkling of how Carson felt, there'd be no stopping her. In fact, she'd probably move in until she was married.

"Hunter tells me he's the detective in charge of Em's case."

"That's right, Mom."

"Such a terrible tragedy." Her mom tsked.

"Unfortunate accidents usually are," Hunter replied.

"Well, I . . ."

Carson jumped in front of her mom, nearly knocking her down. "What do you mean, unfortunate accident?"

Hunter looked surprised.

"Answer my question."

"Carson, honey." Mrs. Johnson put an arm around her. Carson accepted the nurturing touch. "Did you hear what he said, Mrs. J?"

"Carson," Hunter replied, "the case has been closed. We ruled it an accidental drowning."

"Drowning! You can't be serious."

"I'm sorry, Carson," Hunter said.

"No. You're wrong." She looked at Mr. and Mrs. Johnson. "I don't understand. How can you accept that?"

"Carson, let it go. It's over," Mrs. Johnson pleaded.

"Mrs. J?" She couldn't believe what she was hearing. "He doesn't know Emily like we do." She sneered at Hunter. "He's just a cookie-cutter cop."

"Carson. That's enough," her mother scolded.

"No. Emily didn't drown, she was an awesome swimmer, not to mention a champion surfer." She looked around at them all. They actually believed Emily had gotten drunk and then drowned in the lake.

For the first time in five days, she felt tears well up behind her eyes. "You all can think what you want. But I know her death was no accident. And since the local police won't do anything about it, I'll prove it on my own."

Carson stalked toward the parking lot. She hadn't even taken a dozen steps before she was spun around and found herself face to chest with Hunter.

"What exactly do you think you're going to accomplish?"

She cocked her head back and defiantly met his crystal, blue-eyed gaze. "What you and your other cronies couldn't seem to do."

"Carson," he sighed. "I'm sure that this has been hard on you. But it was an accident, plain and simple."

"How can you be so sure?"

"Because I've been doing this for a better part of ten years. The autopsy came back that the cause of death was drowning. It also stated that her blood alcohol content was way over the legal limit."

"So you put two and two together; and as far as you're concerned, that's all there is, right?"

"That is all there is."

"Thank you for your coply advice. Like I said, if you don't want to help me, I'll figure it out on my own." She walked away again.

"Carson. Don't do anything stupid."

"The only thing stupid I've done lately was actually believe you were an all-right guy."

To think she actually contemplated sleeping with that man. Now her only goal was to find Emily's killer and make Detective Reeves a laughing stock.

Chapter 4

Carson forgot her mother was behind her and almost slammed the apartment door in her face.

"Sorry, Mom," she said as she kicked her shoes off in the hallway leading into the living room. Carson had her dress pulled over her head before she reached the bedroom and tossed it on the floor.

Carson dragged out her baggy MTSU sweatshirt and the faded jeans she'd stolen from her skinny brother years ago. After wrestling them on, she was out the door to the living room. She plopped down on the couch, contemplating her next move.

"Carson," her mom called from the kitchen, "we need to go shopping. You have nothing to eat in this place."

"Mom, I have plenty of food in there."

"Yeah, if you're a rabbit." Her mother walked into the living room. "Honestly, Carson, you're getting too thin. Is it money, dear? I'll pay for the groceries."

She looked at her mother. At five feet eight, pushing two hundred pounds, she thought everyone was too thin.

"I like the food in there. And I'm not too thin, Mother. I'm five four and weigh a hundred and thirty-two pounds." Not that she was keeping count. "If anything, I need to lose a few pounds."

"Oh pooh. You don't need to lose any more weight." Her mom smiled. "Now let's talk about that young man Hunter."

"Let's not, Mother."

"He is just a doll. Unlike that boy Jack."

Carson rolled her eyes. "Mom, you liked Jack. In fact you got mad when we broke up." She shook her head. Her mom loved all the guys she'd dated, until the relationship ended. Then she'd find a million and one reasons why they weren't good enough for her daughter.

"Oh, nonsense." She waved her hand in the air. "I think you should give that Hunter a call."

"Forget it, Mother. If you haven't noticed, I don't particularly like the guy, and I don't think he likes me either." Before her mother could utter a syllable, she cut her off. "Case closed."

Only a few more days, Carson thought, and her mother would be gone.

"Carson, I really think—"

"I can't do this." Carson jumped up and rushed into the kitchen. She went to the pantry, grabbed a handful of Ziploc bags, and stuffed them into her sweatshirt.

"Carson, what are you doing?" Her mom joined her in the kitchen.

"Mom, I have to go out for a little bit."

"Okay, I'll come with you."

"I have to do something at work," she lied.

"What am I supposed to do?"

"Watch TV or something." Carson grabbed her purse and headed toward the door.

"You're just like your father. Leaving me alone and gallivanting around. And you expect me to watch TV all day. I could have done this in Florida," she yelled as Carson closed the door.

Indian summer, Carson loved them. Here it was October, and she, driving down the highway with the corvette's top down. Glancing down at the speedometer, she noticed she was pushing seventy-five and let off on the gas pedal. She half-expected to see Hunter Reeves coming after her. No, she wouldn't think of him anymore and the acute pain she felt from his broken promise to help her find Em's killer.

Knots formed in Carson's stomach as she came to her exit. The lake used to be one of her favorite places. A hideaway of sorts when she needed to be alone to think. She vowed never to step foot here again, but Hunter Reeves left her no choice. Emily was murdered, and it was up to Carson to prove it and clear her name. She knew Emily would do the same for her.

Carson drove a few more miles down the road before she noticed the BP gas station on her right, which meant she missed her turnoff.

With no cars coming either way, she whipped a shitty in the middle of the road, proceeded half a mile, saw the exit, and made a right turn onto it. She drove up the winding road, admiring the beautiful houses nestled between trees and hills. The road snaked uphill, hit a plateau before the next mile stretch descended, and eventually evened out just before reaching the lake. She reached the cutoff point, parked her car on the side, and then hiked a quarter of a mile to the lake.

Not once had she felt uncomfortable here, but with the leaves almost gone from the trees and no one on the trail, it gave her the heebie-jeebies.

Carson walked to the edge of the water. The police tape was still secured. A sharp gust of wind blew out of nowhere, swirling the leaves around Carson's ankles. The sudden drop in temperature sent a cold chill through Carson. A dank, cold, musty smell filled the air. Was that death that Carson smelled? Her stomach churned as she thought of that smell being the last scent Emily breathed in. She looked into the quiet, deadly water that claimed her best friend's life and wondered exactly where they had found Em. If only the trees could talk. She'd bet they'd seen what had happened to her best friend.

She shook the ugly thoughts out of her mind. She was here to find clues, not that she had the first idea on how to do it or what she was looking for. But she'd seen enough *NYPD Blue*, *Law and Order*, as well as *Murder She Wrote* episodes to know the police always looked for clues. Carson pulled a Ziploc baggie out of her shirt. She didn't want to taint any evidence that she'd find. She knew she had to find something, anything.

The police rope wound through a few bushes, around a pine tree, across the asphalt, and back, ending at the edge of the water.

She squatted, picked up a nearby branch, and flicked through the dried leaves, hoping to find something. After a minute, she saw something shiny. She reached into her jacket and pulled out a pair of tweezers she brought and dug it out. Disappointment filled her when it turned out to be a dime. She picked it up made a wish and threw it into the lake.

Satisfied that she had exhausted that spot, she moved to another thicket of trees inside the crime tape and started pushing through that area. She came up short again. *Think, Carson, think like a killer.* Dropping to her knees, she began digging into the semisoft, muddish dirt. A few potato bugs and an inch of dirt under her nails later, Carson came up empty-handed. With the back of her hand, she swiped the sweat off her brow, leaving a trail of dirt. She stood up to work the kinks out of her back, unwilling to let a few aches and pains deter her from her objective.

"There's got to be something here," she spoke aloud. "Come on, Emily. Send me a clue. Help me find your killer." Silence was her answer.

Frustrated and on the verge of giving up, she heard the sudden crackle of someone walking on the brush. Her head snapped up, and she spotted a little boy standing between the trees. How long had he been there? Had he watched her this whole time?

"Hi there," she said as she stood. He was adorable with his blond curly hair and huge green eyes. "What's your name?" She took a few steps toward the boy.

The child, who couldn't have been more than six years old, spun around, charging across the old wooden bridge and farther into the woods.

"Wait!" Carson chased after him. "I won't hurt you." By the time she crossed the bridge, the boy was nowhere in sight.

Carson stopped, wondering who he was. Her instinct usually proved to be right, and now it was screaming at her. She'd been sorry in the past when she ignored them, and she was sure that boy was important to her case. Looks as though she'd be making it a habit to visit the lake often.

She headed back across the wooden bridge then stopped, placed her hands on the bridge's rail, and peered over the side, watching as a light wind sent ripples across the lake. How many times had she and Em just sat on this bridge, talking about boys, gossiping about girls?

"Oh, Em . . . ," she spoke to the water. "How could you have drowned here? Why? Who would possibly want you dead? It's not fair," she bellowed.

Carson left the bridge more determined than ever to find some type of clue. It would be getting dark soon. Maybe she had a flashlight in her car. As she headed back to her car, she stopped short at the sight of Hunter Reeves leaning against it. An awful sense of déjà vu ran through her. What was he doing here?

"So, Detective, did you come here to take me to the station again?"

"What are you doing here, Carson?"

"Taking a walk along the lake. What are you doing here, Detective?" She raised her eyebrows.

"I come here a lot. It helps me unwind."

"It's all yours." Pissed that she'd have to cut her sleuthing short, she yanked the keys out of her front pocket.

"Please get away from my car, Detective Reeves."

"Carson, what are you doing here?"

"If you tell me why you're here, I'll tell you why I'm here."

"What are you, five?"

Carson shrugged her shoulders. "Maybe." She didn't care that she was being immature. Why did the man get so under her skin?

"Well?"

"Well, what?" Hunter asked.

"Why are you here?"

"I told you I come here to think."

"You know what, Detective, it's getting late; and it's been an awful long day and I'm exhausted." She nudged him aside and opened her car door. Carson slid behind the wheel, started the engine, and put it in gear. Suddenly, he leaned over the driver's side.

"What were you looking for, Carson?"

"You're the detective, you figure it out. You better move if you want to keep your toes." She started to reverse.

He jumped back before she made good on her promise. "Carson, I'm not your enemy."

Her response was a smile and quick wave of her hand as she turned the car around; then just for spite, she floored it, leaving dust in her wake and in his face. She laughed for the first time in days.

By the time she reached Highway 65, the laughter disappeared. She hadn't found anything to help your theory. Was Hunter right? Could Emily just gotten drunk and drowned?

"Stop it. Don't think like that." She berated herself. She stopped by the gas station, a block from her apartment, and bought a six-pack of beer and some chips.

Carson opened the door to her apartment and almost tripped over the suitcase in the middle of her already-too-narrow hallway.

"It's about time you got back," her mother said. "I thought I was going to have to call a cab or walk to the airport."

"Mom, what are you talking about?" Carson stepped over the suitcase and went into the kitchen. "You don't leave for another couple of days." God, she was tired. She just wanted to drink her beer, veg out on the couch in front of the TV, and watch *Inside the NFL*. Maybe watching highlights of her team—the New York Giants—could take her mind off the fact that Hunter ruined her investigation and the fact that her mother was driving her insane.

"Since I wasn't appreciated here, I changed my flight. Lucky for me, they had seats still available on the nine-thirty flight."

Carson looked at her watch. It was eight fifteen. "Mom, that's crazy. Change your flight back."

"I can't. Your father has already left for the Tampa airport."

Carson eyed the cold beers then reluctantly put them in the refrigerator.

"Let's go," Carson sighed.

She went down the hallway, picked up her mother's suitcase, and headed to her car.

By the time she returned home, she was beyond tired. She grabbed a beer, took one sip, decided she didn't want it, and crawled into bed.

She'd dozed off when the phone rang. There was no nightstand, so the phone sat on the floor. Carson reached down and picked up the receiver.

"Hello."

"Carson."

"Jack, it's late."

"I just heard about Emily. Why didn't you tell me? I should have been there for you."

"I'm sorry I didn't tell you about Em, Jack. It's been really hectic. It didn't even cross my mind to call."

"Are you okay?" he asked.

"I'm getting better."

"Why don't I come over? I miss you."

"Jack, I was just about asleep when you called." She didn't need this right now.

"I don't think you need to be alone at a time like this. You need to be with someone who cares about you."

"Jack, I'm fine. I just need to get some sleep."

"Well, how about this? I need some comfort too. You know I considered her a friend."

Guilt, he was so good at it, but it wasn't going to work. "I know she was your friend, but I need to sleep. I haven't done much of that lately."

"Okay, not tonight," he relented. "Can we at least get together this weekend? Maybe have a drink and reminiscence about some of the things the three of us got into."

"Sure," she said. Anything to get him off the phone. "I'll call you later." She hung up.

Before she could settle back into the bed, the phone rang again. This time she wasn't going to be nice.

"Look, Jack—"

"Is Jack your boyfriend?" the voice asked.

Carson sat up. "No, Detective Reeves, I don't have a boyfriend." Not that it was any of his business, she thought. "Is there something you wanted?" The other end was silent. "Hello, are you still there?"

"Did you find anything at the lake today?" he asked.

"What do you care? You basically think my friend killed herself." Carson paused. "Or are you having second thoughts about your theory?" A shiver of hope ran down her spine.

"Did you find anything or not?"

"Answer my question first!"

"Carson, I haven't changed my opinion."

"I guess that's the end of this conversation."

Before she could hang up, he said, "Unless you found something that might change it for me."

She didn't know what he was up to, so she decided not to tell him about the little boy she'd seen. He'd probably laugh at her anyway if she told him all she had was her gut instinct.

"I didn't find anything. So you can rest easy about breaking your promise. Good-bye, Detective."

"Carson, listen. The Johnsons asked me not to tell you this. The main reason Emily went to Hawaii was to get away from her parents. They were threatening to put her in rehab. She had a drinking problem."

"Liar." She slammed down the receiver then threw the phone across the room.

Chapter 5

It was Carson's first day back to work in almost a week. She had a fresher outlook, and it felt good to be on the job. It wasn't that she hated her work; lately, she just felt there was something else out there for her. Too bad, she didn't know what it was.

After she punched in, she walked to the coffee grinder, ground enough beans for a pot, and brewed coffee. As she heard the front door swing open, she looked up. It was Peter Boston. What was he doing here on Thursday?

"Great," she murmured. "There goes having a semigood day."

"Hello, Carson." He stared a second then cleared his throat. "I'm really sorry to hear about your friend."

"Thank you," she said, a little shocked.

"I didn't expect to see you so soon. You could have taken more time, you know?"

What was going on? He was actually being human. She was almost tempted to pull on his face to make sure that it wasn't somebody else wearing a mask of Peter.

"No. I needed to get back to work."

"Well, if you need anything, let us know." He walked back into the kitchen.

She peeked around the corner to make sure he hadn't vanished and that she hadn't dreamed the conversation.

Although it felt good to be back to work, a few hours into the shift, Carson became anxious. She needed the money, but she needed to find Emily's killer more.

With no one at the bar and lunch basically over, she decided to count her measly tips. She pulled out the ones and counted them, came up with thirty—more than she expected—then traded them for big bills. She stuffed the money into her pocket.

After the relief bartender arrived, Carson jumped in her car, headed down Highway 65 toward downtown Nashville, then took Forty to Twenty-first Avenue exit. She drove down Twenty-first Avenue for a few miles then pulled into a parking lot of a white three-story brick office building.

Carson entered through the rear entrance and decided she needed the exercise, so she took the stairs to the third floor. Once she reached it, she headed to the end of the hall and barged through the door marked BJ's Investigations.

No one sat behind the desk. But grunting sounds came from the office down the hall. He was either moving furniture or indulging in a little afternoon delight. She'd bet money on the latter.

BJ wasn't expecting her, and she knew how much he hated surprises. They had met freshman year in English class. Their friendship had spawned after a boring first date. Once they decided never to date again, they'd become inseparable. They still kept in touch, but through the years, it had become less frequent.

"BJ," she called out, "it's Carson."

The office went silent; then she heard some movement and a string of filthy curses. BJ came out of the office.

"Carson, what a surprise." He gave her a big bear hug and a peck on the cheek. "How are you?"

"I'm hanging in there. And yourself?" She tried not to laugh at his attempt at fixing himself. His tie was still askew, and he forgot to zip his pants.

"Can't complain, business is good. A little slow at the moment." He yanked at her apron. "Still bartending, I see."

"It pays the bills."

"My offer still stands. With some hard-core training, we can get your PI license. We'd make a great team."

For the first time, his offer sounded appealing, but she had never needed this kind of help before.

Hopefully this would be the only time.

"That's kind of why I'm here."

"Really. You've decided to become a PI? That's great."

"Not exactly."

"I don't understand."

"I need your expertise." She told him all about Emily, how the police were closing the case and ruling it an accident. She left out the information about her blood alcohol and the lie Hunter told her the night before about Em's parents putting her in rehab.

"Wow." He ran a hand through his hair. "Shit, Emily's dead. You've had a hell of a week."

"If you could just give me some pointers. Tell me what I should look for. Whom to talk to? That sort of stuff." She knew she should hire him, but she really didn't have that kind of money to spare. And this was too personal. She had to be part of it.

"Of course, I'll help you," BJ replied. "What I'd like to do is have a look at her police report first. Then I can better gauge what to look for."

"Great, so you're telling me you can't help me."

"No, I'm not saying that."

"But you said you need her police report."

"And I can get it."

"Oh."

"I'll pick it up. I'm not sure how long it will take me. But go home and wait for me there."

"Oh, thank you." She gave him another hug.

"Just have a cold one waiting for me and a pizza with sausage and pepperoni."

"You got it." They left his office together.

They chatted about nothing as they made way to the cars. Since his was closer, Carson walked that direction with him. She told him about her mom's latest visit while he threw all his stuff in the trunk. He was just about to shut it when something shiny caught her eye. She reached for it, but he grabbed her hand.

"Don't touch that."

"You carry a gun?"

"Yes." He dropped her hand and then slammed the trunk. "Some jobs are riskier than others."

"So how do I go about getting a gun?" she asked.

"You don't."

"But I'm looking for a murderer. That's pretty dangerous. God, what am I doing?" She sat on the car's bumper. "I need a gun."

"You don't need a gun."

"Yes, I do. I'm looking for a killer."

"I doubt you'll find a killer." He scoffed.

"What does that mean?" Carson looked up at him, but he refused to meet her gaze.

"You don't believe me either?" She stood up. "Why did you say you'd help me? You're just like all the rest. I thought you, of all people, would believe in me."

"I just—"

"Stop humoring me." She punched him in the gut.

"Dammit, Carson." He rubbed his belly. "You still pack a mean punch."

"Don't bother with the police report." She rubbed her knuckles as she headed toward her car.

Carson took her time answering the knock on her door. Looking through the peephole, she sighed then opened the door. "What do you want, BJ?"

"I need a beer." He walked past her, headed into the kitchen, pulled out a beer, twisted off the top, and took a swig.

"I thought you said it was a closed case," he asked.

She followed him to the kitchen. "You went to the police station? Why?"

"Because." He waved his beer in the air. "Now about the case being closed?"

"That's what I was told. They ruled her death accidental."

"And you forgot to mention the fact that Hunter Reeves is the detective in charge."

"You know Hunter?" Her voice cracked.

BJ took one look at her face and said, "Oh brother." He took another sip of his beer. "Don't tell me you have the hots for him. Are you sleeping with him?"

"What? Of course I'm not. And no, I don't have the hots for him. I don't even like him. Why would you think I was sleeping with him?"

"Let's just say that Hunter has a way with women, and plenty of them. So it's a good thing you're not doing the wild thing."

"You seem to know a lot about the guy."

"He's probably the best cop in Nashville. In my line of work, I tend to rely on the police force a lot. I scratch their back, and every once in a while, they'll throw me a bone. Except this time." He opened the pizza box, pulled off a semiwarm slice, folded it, and took a bite.

"What does that mean?"

He washed the pizza down with another swig of beer. "It means, I couldn't get the file. For some reason, Hunter wouldn't let me look at it. And he wasn't too happy that I asked."

"Did he say why?"

"Darling, he doesn't have to tell me anything."

"Does he know that you were doing it for me?"

"I didn't tell him. But now that I think about it, he was mumbling something about what the hell did she think she was doing. I guess he was talking about you."

"Jerk, he's probably doing this just to spite me."

"No. That's not it at all. Hunter's too good of a cop. I think there's more to it. You might be onto something." He put his beer on the counter. "I'm sorry I doubted you."

She stared at BJ. "Why did you?"

"It's not important."

"It's important to me."

Ignoring her, BJ said, "The only thing that matters right now is getting that file."

Carson decided not to push; besides, he was right. They needed Emily's file.

"You think that Hunter changed his mind and believes me. But why wouldn't he just tell me that instead of making me go through all this." She waved her hand.

"I'd say that he's not the type of man to admit that he could be wrong. Especially if he's admitting it to a woman."

"And he's still at the station?" Carson asked.

"He was when I left. Why?"

Carson grabbed her keys. "I believe it's time our friendly Detective Hunter admit that he was wrong."

"Carson, wait."

"Stay as long as you like, BJ. I'll probably call you tomorrow to get some more help."

Carson jumped in her car and flew down the highway. Within ten minutes, she pulled in the police station parking lot, got out of her car, and slammed the car door. Her blood was boiling. She didn't know if it was because Hunter had changed his mind about Emily or that he had likely slept with half the women in Nashville.

She scanned the police parking lot, looking for his blue sedan. Luckily for her, there was only one there. She hoped it was the right one. Her plan was to lean by the car—like he did to her that night—until he left the station. Her plan was thwarted the minute she leaned against it and the alarm went off. Before she could blink half, the precinct—or so it seemed—rushed out with guns drawn.

"Hands in the air," was shouted at her from all directions.

She threw her hands upward and prayed they wouldn't shoot her.

"What the—"

"Hunter." Her eyes met his aquamarine ones. Relief flooded her veins at the sight of Hunter.

"It's all right, everyone. I'll take it from here." Hunter holstered his gun. The other officers relaxed and put down their weapons.

Hunter walked up to the car. "You can put your hands down now."

Slowly, Carson brought her trembling arms down to her sides.

"What the hell are you doing messing around with my car? And at a police station to boot?"

"I wasn't doing anything to your car. And since when does leaning against a car require the police force?"

"It seems we have a ballsy car theft in the area. We've lost a couple of cars the past month. Why am I telling you this?" He rubbed his hand down his face. "What are you doing here?"

Carson brushed her hair behind her ear. "Waiting for you."

"Really." He had moved to stand in front of her. "Why?" He placed his hands on both sides of her shoulders, pinning her against the car.

Now she knew why BJ had thought she might have slept with him. His intent aquamarine eyes mesmerized her. And his body was so close she could almost feel the heat of it.

She swallowed audibly. "I . . ."

"You?"

She didn't think it was possible, but he moved even closer. His breath smelled like peppermint. He brought his left hand away from the car and brought it up to caress her cheek.

"Damn, but you are cute," he whispered right before his lips descended on hers.

She knew the kiss was coming, had expected it by the look in his eyes, but she wasn't prepared for the expertise of his tongue as it meshed with her own. It was like he was teaching her to dance. One step then two steps back, one step then a twirl. She was so shaken by the time he ended the kiss that if he hadn't had her pinned to the car, she would have sunk to the ground.

He trailed kisses from the corner of her mouth down to her neck and back up to her ear. "If you give me a few minutes, I'll be out of here, and we can go back to my house," he whispered in her ear.

Still dazed by the kiss, she said, "Hunter, I need—"

"What? What do you need?" His tongue darted into her ear.

She sighed. "I need Em's case file."

"Son-of-a-bitch." He pulled away from her. "So that's what this is all about."

Her eyes flew open at his quick departure. She knew the kiss made her look manipulative, but she didn't care.

He raked his hands through his blond hair. "BJ put you up to this, didn't he? I knew PIs got away with some sleazy stuff, but this takes the cake. I'm going to kick his ass."

"BJ didn't put me up to anything."

He dropped his hand from his hair. "So seducing me was your idea?"

"Seduce you," she yelled. "If anything, you seduced me."

"Give me a break. You show up at my job, waiting for me. You flash those sexy big hazel eyes of yours my way. Then you use that soft throaty voice and call out my name, 'Hunter,'" he squeaked out with a high-raised voice to demonstrate.

"What was I suppose to say when you and your squad room full of goons came racing out with their guns pointed, ready to shoot me. An innocent civilian, I might add. And I don't talk like that." She fisted her hands on her hips.

"Bull. I doubt there's anything innocent about you."

"Oh yeah? I was innocent enough to believe you were a good cop." His face turned deep red. Instead of feeling triumphant at the landed blow, she felt a little scared that she had crossed the line.

Hunter flexed his hands while his mouth moved from the count of one to ten. "I think you should go home."

Carson stomped past him and headed for her car then turned back. "I will find out what happened to Emily with or without your help."

"I wouldn't if I were you. If I hear anything that you've been up to that falls in the category of police work or investigating work, I'll have you in a jail cell so fast your head will spin."

She turned on her heel.

"I mean it, Carson," he yelled before she got in the car.

Her hands shook as she got into her car. She didn't know whether she was coming or going. One minute she had guns turned on her, the next she was being professionally kissed, and then she was threatened with jail time. Her stomach flipped remembering his kiss. Hunter was too dangerous to be around. It was probably for the best letting him believe she kissed him just to get Em's file.

When Carson got home, BJ was asleep on her couch, and there wasn't a beer left.

"BJ, wake up." She shook him.

"What?" He sprung up and looked around the apartment. Shaking his head, he rubbed the sleep from his eyes.

"What time is it?" He yawned.

"It's time for us to go out and get a drink. I don't have to work until tomorrow night."

Still only half-awake, he looked at Carson. "What's the matter? What did that bastard do?"

"Nothing. I'm basically on my own." She refused to look at him.

"Car, I know you. Now tell me what happened."

"Oh, all right. He kissed me, accused me of—"

"Wait, he kissed you?"

"Yep, then accused me of seducing him, which he thought was your idea. But I told him differently. Then he threatened to throw me in jail if I continued to look into Emily's death." She threw her hands in the air and paced.

"He kissed you?"

"Will you stop with that already. It was a stupid, harmless kiss. It didn't mean anything." She headed to the bedroom before he could see she was lying.

"I'll only be a few minutes, and then you're taking me dancing," she called out from the room.

Twenty minutes later, they jumped into Carson's convertible and headed for downtown Nashville.

Thursday night was usually a happening night. It wasn't as crowded as Friday or Saturday, so they wouldn't have to wait in long lines. Better, an older clientele frequented during the week.

They decided to hit the Have a Nice Day Café. It was a throwback to the seventies. The staff dressed disco-style, the walls were covered with movie paraphernalia, and they served drinks called Happy Bowls, an actual fish bowl filled with grain alcohol served with eight straws in grape or fruit punch flavor.

Carson dragged BJ through the front door, past the dance floor to the back bar to a pair of empty stools.

The bartender walked up, leaned over the bar, and planted a big kiss on Carson's lips.

"Carson, sweetie, what's up?" he yelled over the loud music.

"You are, babe." She winked. "Busy tonight, Chris?"

"Nah, it's kind of slow. Who's the new guy?" He eyed BJ.

"This is my good friend, BJ; and no, he's not your type." She smiled.

"Oh well, his loss. What are you drinking?"

"We'll have a grape Happy Bowl."

She looked over at BJ. He looked uncomfortable. "When was the last time you came to a club?"

"It's been awhile," he screamed. "I've kind of outgrown the club scene."

The bartender returned with the drink and placed it between the two of them.

"Here's to your first night back in the club scene." She took a long generous sip out of the fish bowl. "Woo hoo, we are going to have fun tonight." She danced in her chair to the seventies hit "Funky Town."

After the initial sip of the purple drink, BJ switched to beer. He shrugged. "I can't drink that stuff. I have to work in the morning. This is your night. Enjoy it and don't worry about me."

He smiled at her. "I love you, Car."

She kissed him on the cheek. "Thanks, BJ. And I'm sorry about punching you earlier. By the way, have you been working out because that punch really hurt."

"A little." He laughed.

"C'mon, let's dance." She popped off her stool, dragged BJ off his, and barreled them through the crowd to the dance floor.

The music flowed through her body. She twirled around BJ, gyrating her hips; she ran her hands through her hair while undulating her upper body in a slow, rhythmic motion.

They danced together for three more songs. With sweat dripping off both of them, they decided to exit the dance floor when the DJ got it in his head to play a love song. Hunter's seductive smile flashed in her mind. *Not good, Carson.* She returned to her drink and took a long sip, hoping to wash Hunter from her mind. Carson stumbled. She hadn't eaten much today or for the week, so the drink was hitting her a little harder and faster than usual.

"I'm going to the bathroom. I'll be right back."

She muscled her way in the ladies room. There were four stalls and eight women in line. She watched the girls ahead of her. They were paired into groups, all of them laughing and talking about the guys they had picked out for the night. It reminded her of the times she, Em, and Jessie used to go out. Now Jessie was busy with her husband as well as her little one-year-old while Em was gone forever.

Carson suddenly felt the walls closing in on her.

The room started to spin. She raced out of the restroom, across the dance floor, and out the front door. She sucked in big gasps of air then leaned against the building, letting the cold air seep into her bones.

"Carson?"

She lifted her head at the sound of BJ's voice.

"BJ, I want to go home." She fell into his arms.

"Okay." He kept his arm around her as he walked her to the car. He eased her into the passenger's side then ran around and climbed in the driver's side. "You want to talk about it?"

Carson leaned her head against the window. "I miss her and can't imagine never seeing her again." A slight smile formed on her lips. "We were both planning to marry the cutest, richest guys then buy houses next to Jessie, and all of our children would grow up together and be best friends. Now she'll never have children. It's not fair." She closed her eyes.

"I know. Give yourself some time. It's only been five days. It's tough, but you'll get through this, like you do everything else, right, Carson?"

BJ started up the car and took Carson home.

Chapter 6

The sun broke through the thin bedroom window blinds, bathing Carson in a pool of light. "Ugh," she groaned as she rolled away from the unbearable glare and buried her head under the pillow. *Just a few more minutes, then I'll get up,* she chanted in her head. She was on the verge of falling back to sleep when someone pounded at her front door.

"Go away," she mumbled.

She planned to ignore them, but after two more loud knocks, she knew the person wasn't going to go away. She threw her pillow across the room then rolled out of bed. "I'm coming," she yelled as she shuffled her way to the door then pulled it open. BJ stood there with a McDonald's bag in his hand.

"It's about time. Breakfast is probably cold." He walked past her. "Boy." He waved his hand in front of his face. "You didn't drink much, but you smell like a brewery."

Yeah, and her breath tasted like dog doodoo, she thought. "Just be quiet and give me some coffee."

"Here you go, semihot coffee with two creams and two sugars."

She took the cup he offered and wrapped her hands around it. "You are a lifesaver." She pulled the little plastic tab off the cup, took a huge sniff, sighed at the wonderful smell, then had a sip.

"What are you doing here and so early in the morning?"

BJ had walked over to the little round wooden table where he proceeded to extract two breakfast burritos and a couple of Egg McMuffins from the bag.

"I guess you don't remember me telling you I was coming over today to help you become somewhat of a detective."

She shrugged. "I guess I had more sips of that drink than we both thought."

"Here, eat this." He handed her a burrito. "Then take a shower, and we'll talk."

She grabbed the burrito, unwrapped it, took a big bite, then headed into the bathroom.

"And brush your teeth too," he yelled after her.

She flipped him the bird before she closed the bathroom door.

Although she wanted to savor her too-hot shower, she decided to take a quick one. Less than five minutes later, she stepped from the shower. She brushed her teeth two times then got dressed. When she went back into the living room, all evidence of breakfast were gone. BJ was hunched over the table with a pad and pencil, scribbling away.

"What'cha doing?" She peered over his back.

"Just working on some stuff." He flipped the notepad close before she could see any information. "Ready to learn?"

She nodded then sat down at the table next to him.

He handed her the pad and pencil. "Okay. First, you need to write down everything you know about Emily."

"I can't just tell you?"

"No, I need you to write it all down. Her full name, birthday, social security number, the last time you spoke to her, when she left for Hawaii, how long was she there, when did she get back. We could check the airlines for that. Who her friends are, where she lives, her spending habits. You should try to get a hold of her bank statements. Talk to any boyfriends she may have had—

"Why aren't you writing any of this down?" he asked.

She stared at him. "I guess I'm just a little overwhelmed. I really need to know all this information?"

"Yes. Now write."

"But what does all this stuff have to do with her murder?"

"Maybe nothing at all or maybe everything. All we need is to find one little thing that seems out of place, and we catch a lead."

"Okay. You're the PI. I'll do what you say." Carson started to write.

BJ placed his hand atop of hers. "Car."

She stopped writing, his serious tone capturing her full and immediate attention.

"I just want to warn you. You may find out some things about Em you didn't know about her or want to know. You'll probably discover things that will surprise you. People change without us knowing it. No matter how close they are to us. So you have to be willing to go through with this, no matter what. And if you don't think you can handle what you might find out about her, I suggest we don't go any further."

Carson looked into his brown eyes. "I can handle it." She suddenly felt the hairs on her arm stand up and a sinking feeling in her stomach but quickly brushed it aside. She knew Em; they had no secrets, no matter what Hunter had said that night on the phone. He had spooked her, that was all.

"Could you tell me all that stuff again?"

BJ started from the beginning. This time she wrote it all down.

Carson's head was still reeling from everything BJ had told her she needed to discover about Em. It seemed like a lot of annoying and pointless work. Her insides tightened as she pulled into Em's parent's neighborhood.

She'd never been afraid of Em's parents. In fact, there were many times she wished they'd been her parents, but that was neither here nor there.

She had a feeling she was about to breach a friendship. Em's parents wanted to believe Hunter had put an end to the search for why she died. But Carson didn't believe and wouldn't let go. Em deserved that much.

After a few minutes of sitting in the driveway, she worked up enough courage to leave her car. Carson took a deep breath as she knocked on the door. A part of her hoped they weren't home, but that wish was short-lived when Mrs. Johnson opened the door.

"Carson."

"Hello, Mrs. J."

"I'm so glad you're here." Em's mother hugged Carson. "Come in."

Carson stood in the foyer, expecting Em to bounce down the stairs at any moment. She still couldn't believe she was gone. She turned to Mrs. J.

"About . . ."

"Yes, Jim and I had a talk last night. In fact, I was going to call you later today."

"You were?" Hunter's words echoed in Carson's head. "Emily left so her parents couldn't put her in rehab." She felt her anxiety kick up a notch. Were they going to confide in her and confirm Hunter's accusation?

"We weren't very sympathetic to you the other day. I hadn't realized how hard this has been for you. What you must be going through. I always used to say you two were the sisters neither one had. I'm sure you've been under a tremendous strain. You haven't been sleeping. I can see it in your eyes." She brushed Carson's hair behind her ear.

"In time, we know you'll come to accept her death as we have. We just wanted to let you know we're here for you."

Carson's heart sank. This woman that she'd thought of as a second mother for over half her life was now a stranger. An overwhelming need to leave filled Carson. Instead she smiled at Mrs. J and asked, "Mrs. Johnson, this might sound odd, but I was hoping to spend a little time in her room. Pay a little homage to our time as kids." She looked up and noticed tears in the older woman's eyes.

"Mrs. J?"

"No, it's okay. Go on upstairs." Mrs. J left Carson alone in the foyer.

As Carson made her way to the stairs, she stopped to stare into the sitting room.

"Hey, Car, watch this."

"Em, you better not. Your mom will kill you."

"Relax, nothing's going to happen. Here goes."

Carson held her breath as she watched Em perform a backhand spring off the edge of the chair. She about made it when, just like that, her body twisted too far to the left and she careened into her mother's reading table, shattering her priceless antique reading lamp.

"I was never able to fix that lamp."

Carson jumped at the sound of Mrs. J's voice.

"I'm sorry, dear. I didn't mean to startle you.

"It's okay, Mrs. J."

"I thought you might be hungry, so I made your favorite. Peanut butter and bananas with marshmallow whip on toast."

"Thanks." Carson hadn't had one of these in years. She wondered if it had the same appeal as it did when she was thirteen. She took a small bite. Yep, it still was good. She'd make a detour to the store on the way home and pick up a jar of peanut butter along with some marshmallow whip.

Sandwich in hand, she took the stairs at a snail's pace; then she stood in front of the closed door for a few seconds before she flung it open. Em's room still looked as it had fifteen years ago. A white canopy bed piled with stuffed animals sat in the middle of the room, a white vanity with an oval mirror was against the wall in front of the bed, and a white plastic stand that housed a small boom box was on the other wall.

Em had moved back in with her parents a little over a year ago for a few months when she decided to quit her job and pursue her dream to be a professional surfer. Yet she'd never gotten around to making any changes.

Carson wasn't sure what she was looking for, but she was sure she'd know what it was once she found it.

She stood in front of the oval mirror, its surface crowded with taped pictures. She pulled off her own graduation picture, turned it over and read her words of promise to be friends forever, then slowly put it back and looked at the others. There was a picture of them in their pom-pom uniforms, the day Em had won homecoming queen, another of them when they where twelve and played on the same softball team. Carson took that one, putting it in her purse.

She looked at the last picture. Prom night. Carson was with someone she thought was a friend but turned out to be an octopus, rendering her prom night short. Em was with Teddy, her first true love.

Carson had forgotten all about Teddy. Did he even know what happened to Em? He wasn't at the funeral. She had to find him and tell him. Even though they'd broken up years ago, Carson was sure that Teddy would want to know. She hadn't talked to him since college. She hadn't a clue what he was up to or where he lived.

A sudden chill filled the room, and she could have sworn she was no longer alone. Instead of feeling spooked, she felt sadness.

She believed in ghosts and supernatural phenomenon. No one knew it, but Carson owned every season of *Buffy*, *Angel*, *Charmed*, and *Supernatural* on DVD.

"Em," she whispered, "I know you are there, and you don't need to worry. I'm going to find out who did this to you and make them pay."

Just like that, the chill was gone.

Carson searched through the vanity to no avail. Next, she went to the small closet, ignoring the clothes; her hand glided across the shelf until she bumped up to something hard. She grabbed a hold of it and brought it down. Em's high school yearbook. She began to open it then stopped, knowing she could easily spend the next hour reading what everybody wrote. Putting it back, Carson discovered another book, a diary. She stuck it in her purse.

She wandered over to the white plastic stand and took a look at Em's book collection—well, maybe not a collection since there were only five books. One happened to be Carson's favorite book, *Rebecca*, that had been missing for years. All this time, she thought she had lost it. She picked up the book and was about to put it in her purse when she remembered she had replaced her missing copy a few months ago.

Still, the book was hers. She'd highlighted favorite passages, made notes in the margins as well as the name of the boy who she wanted to be her Maxim. With the page memorized, she flipped to it. Not only had the name been cut out, but there was a letter folded into the page.

She pulled it out. The envelope had no name, only a PO Box. The PO Box was right in Franklin. She opened it up and read the letter.

My Precious Emily,

I can't believe we have found each other once again. Seeing you in Hawaii was fate. We were meant to be together forever. Not a day has gone by that I didn't picture your beautiful face. I can't wait until next week to see you again and make love to you.

Until then, my love.

There was no signature. Carson looked at the envelope. There was no return address. She almost dropped the letter when she looked at the postmark. It had been dated the week of Em's death.

Em had been home that whole week, and Carson hadn't known. Why? Did her parents? No, they couldn't have known, not if they'd plan to send her to rehab. And who was this mysterious lover? Had he known she was back?

Carson stuffed the letter into her purse. She raced down the stairs, almost knocking Mrs. Johnson on her rear-end as well as spilling the contents of her purse across the floor.

"Mrs. J, I'm so sorry. Are you all right?" Carson quickly bent down to pick up her stuff, not wanting Em's mother to see the letter or diary.

"I think so. Are you okay? Why were you running like there was a fire? Here, let me help you."

"No! I mean, it's okay, I've got it." Carson tucked everything safely into her purse. "I'm about to be late for work."

She noticed the worried look in Mrs. J's eyes. *Great, she thinks I'm crazy*, Carson muttered in her head. She gave Mrs. J a quick hug then headed to the door, but she couldn't leave without turning back to ask, "Did you know that Em was back in town?"

"No." She shook her head. "If we had known she was coming to town, we would have postponed our trip."

"Your trip?"

"Yes. We had decided to get away for a few days. Spend some time in our cabin at Mount Eagle, watch the leaves change. I could have sworn we told Emily all about it."

Carson had no doubt that Em knew. It explained how she was able to be here without anyone knowing.

"What's with the questions, Carson?"

"I don't know." She shrugged. "I just wonder why she didn't tell me or you she was home. Then maybe she'd still be here."

"Oh, Carson, don't do this to yourself." Em's mother stepped toward her.

"I gotta go, Mrs. J."

"Promise me you'll keep in touch. Maybe we can do lunch next week."

"Sure thing," Carson said halfheartedly, sure that once Mrs. J found out what she was up to, she'd want no part of her.

Chapter 7

Carson had a half hour before her shift started, so she decided to have something to eat. As usual, she opted for the chicken salad; lately, she'd become a creature of habit.

She almost dropped her fork when Jack sat across from her—speaking of bad habits. He was one habit she kept trying to break.

"Jack, what are you doing here?"

"I came to get a drink."

"Well, the bar's over there." She used her fork to point it out, didn't realize there was food on it, and flicked lettuce on Jack's face.

"Thanks, but I'm not hungry." He peeled the lettuce off his cheek.

"Oh, Jack, I'm so sorry." She looked into her salad bowl and broke out in laughter.

"Okay, it wasn't that funny."

"You're right." She looked up at him, pictured the lettuce stuck to his cheek, and once again erupted in laughter.

She wasn't sure if it was lack of sleep or the circumstances surrounding the past week that had her in hysterics.

"It's not funny anymore," Jack warned.

"Ohhh god." She wiped the tears from her eyes, drew a steadying breath, and met his disgruntled gaze.

"Now will you listen to what I have to say?"

"Go ahead," she squeaked.

"I'm out of here." He got up and stormed away.

"Jack, I'm sorry, but I can't help it. Fine, you big baby." Jeez, he was awfully temperamental these days. What he needed was thicker skin like Hunter. Damn, she needed to quit thinking about the pompous Casanova.

She threw her salad away then went into the employee bathroom, brushed her teeth then put on her lipstick.

Carson left the bathroom and headed into the kitchen to the office. She looked through the office window; it was empty. She tried the door and found it unlocked; so she went in, pulled the letter out of her purse, and made a copy. Once she finished, she headed out to the bar to work.

Happy hour was a little light that evening. Carson suspected it was due to the football game the next day. UT was playing its biggest rival, Alabama, in Alabama. So a lot of people decided to head to the next state and catch the game.

She went to the end of the bar to greet the customer who just sat down.

"Hi there, what can I get you?" Carson smiled her most welcoming smile.

"Do you know how to make a Harvey Wallbanger?" His tongue rolled his toothpick in and out of his mouth.

"Yes." Carson rolled her eyes. She didn't really need an obnoxious customer.

She grabbed a glass, filled it with ice, poured a shot of her cheapest vodka, squeezed fresh OJ to the top, then topped it off with Galliano, stuck a straw in it, and put it in front of him.

"Would you like to start a tab, sir?"

"No."

"That'll be five dollars."

He handed her a crumbled five-dollar bill from his pocket.

"My name's Carson, if you need anything else." She took his money and rang up the drink.

She barely closed the register before he called her name. With a smile, she turned to him. "Yes?"

"I thought you said you knew how to make a Harvey Wallbanger?"

"I do."

"Then what do you call this?"

"A Harvey Wallbanger."

"So you don't know how to make one?"

"No, maybe you don't know what one tastes like," she shot back. Damn. In the twelve years she'd been in the business, she never berated a guest.

"I want to speak to a manager right now."

She left the bar to find Walt. Unfortunately for her, the only one available was Peter.

"Peter, there's a guy at the bar that wants to talk to a manager." Carson pointed to the jerk.

"Hello, sir, my name is Peter Boston. What's the problem?"

"She is." He pointed to Carson. "She has an attitude problem, and she doesn't know the first thing about making a drink."

"I'm sorry, sir. We won't charge you for the drink, and why don't you let us make you another one."

"Okay. But I want him to make it." He pointed to Kyle, the other bartender.

Carson watched Kyle make the exact same drink that she made. With her arms crossed over her chest, she watched the man take a sip and waited to hear his complaint.

"Perfect," he claimed.

She dropped her arms to her sides. "That's the same."

"Carson," Peter warned, "can I talk to you for a moment?"

She followed Peter outside to the deserted patio. Carson rubbed her hands up and down her arms to ward of the chill.

"I want you to go home."

"What? You can't be serious? That guy's a jerk."

He held up his hand to stop her tirade. "You know the motto. The guest is always right."

"But . . ."

"No, Carson. I was right yesterday when I said it was too soon for you to come back. And the only reason I'm going to tolerate this type of behavior is because of your loss. Take the next few days off, get it together, and come back to work on Monday." He left.

"Shit, shit, shit." She kicked the building. "So much for thinking you turned human, Peter." She sat down on the bench and took in five deep breaths to tamper her anger. Carson never had more than a few days off unless she was on vacation. What would she do with herself? Wait, this was the best thing that could have happened. Now she could work on Em's case.

*   *   *

Carson checked her makeup once more in the rearview mirror before getting out of her car. She pulled on the pant legs of her jeans, getting the cuff to sit atop her sandals. There was a slight breeze. She was glad she opted to bring a sweater.

She took a deep breath then pushed open the door to the smoke-filled sports bar. Not much action going on here tonight either. The place had fifteen TVs, and only one showed the World Series. Then again, she wasn't surprised; Tennessee didn't have much use for baseball since they didn't have a team. It had been one of the drawbacks when she moved there at the age of twelve—no professional sports. But Tennessee had improved the past five years. They now had a football team and a hockey team. She hoped they'd get a baseball team.

She pulled her eyes away from the baseball game to look around the bar. He wasn't here. She decided that was a good thing. It was foolish of her to have set up the meeting. Without hesitation, she backed out of the bar; but before she could turn around, she bumped into something very hard and male.

"Change your mind?" Hunter's arms tightened around her.

Carson pulled away from his grasp. "No," was all she managed.

"Then why don't we get a table." He maneuvered them toward a secluded booth in the back of the bar.

Carson wasn't sure how to take that. Either he wanted to be alone with her, or he didn't want to be seen with her. Then realizing her thoughts, she pushed the crazy ideas out of her mind.

She slipped into the booth and felt a twinge of jealousy as the waitress directed her attention to Hunter. "What can I get for you?" she purred.

"I'll have a beer, whatever you have on draft."

"One draft coming up," she replied as she began to leave.

"I'll have the same," Carson called before she got too far away. She felt a little triumph when the waitress turned back, red-faced. That'll teach the little twit not to be rude and ignore her.

Carson looked back at Hunter. A smile showed his perfect white teeth.

"What?"

"Are you always this feisty? Or is it just when you're around me?" he asked.

"Huh. I guess you missed the part where the girl completely ignored me."

"I'm sure it wasn't intentional. She seems a little busy."

"Whatever." Carson rolled her eyes. "I'm in the business, remember. She's not that busy. Besides, she did it on purpose. The girl only had eyes for you." She knew she sounded calm, but inside, she was pissed off by the invisible treatment.

"I'm sure if you play your cards right, she'd give you her number," Carson added.

"You think so?" Hunter turned to the bar to search for the cocktail waitress.

"I didn't ask you here to talk about your sex life." She needed to focus on why she was here. Not on Hunter and his latest conquests.

He smiled as he gave her his full attention. "I have to admit, I was a little surprised to hear from you after our last meeting." His eyes strayed to her lips.

Just as she'd been surprised to his quick agreement to meet with her after the crack she had made about his cop skills. Not to mention that if they hadn't had the argument, she might have done the unthinkable and landed herself in his bed. She ignored the flutter in her stomach.

"I've found something that I think you should look at." She pulled the letter from her purse and handed it to him.

As he took it from her, the waitress appeared with their beers. She lingered a little too long at their table, and Carson couldn't believe she was actually flirting with Hunter right in front of his date. Not that they we're on a date, but the little twit didn't know that.

Carson shifted her gaze to Hunter. Was he enjoying this flirtation? The girl couldn't be more than eighteen, twenty at the most, but everything looked tight and perky on her.

Carson glanced at her own breasts. They were still going strong for a thirty-year-old, at least in her eyes, but what would Hunter think?

Disgusted with her thoughts, she picked up her beer and took a long drink.

A half beer later, the waitress was gone, and Hunter was still perusing the letter. She watched him, looking for anything that gave his thoughts away, but there was nothing.

A minute later, he stared at her. "Where did you get this?"

"It doesn't matter."

"Yes, it does matter. Since it's not addressed to you, I have to believe it was obtained illegally."

"As a matter of fact, it wasn't. I found it in a book that I loaned Em." It wasn't all a lie. The book was hers.

"And you just happened . . ." He took a swig of his beer. "You know what? Never mind. I don't want to know." He sighed.

"So what are we going to do about it?"

"We aren't going to do anything about it."

"I don't believe this. Here I bring you proof that something's not right. And still, you don't believe me."

He grabbed her hand before she could get up and leave. "Has it occurred to you that if you're right, then that means there's a killer out there? And you could be putting yourself in danger? That you might get killed?"

No, she hadn't thought about any of that. Her only thought was to see justice done for Emily. "That's why I've come to you for help, again."

"Then stay out of it."

"I can't."

"You don't know the first thing about catching a killer. I doubt you even know how to defend yourself."

"I'll have you know that I'm a green belt in tae kwon do." Not that it meant a whole lot. The first thing her teacher told her was it was good to know the art, but if she ever found herself in a dire situation, her best bet was to run.

"There you have it. You're ready to go out and catch a killer. And to think I thought you could be in danger." He finished his beer then waved to the waitress, pointed to the empty glass, and signaled for two more.

He leaned across the table. "Have you ever been held at gunpoint?"

She raised an eyebrow.

"That day at the station doesn't count. You weren't in any real danger. How about being held at knifepoint?"

"Scaring me isn't going to work," she lied.

"Well, it ought to. This isn't a game. It's real life. So why don't you go back to work behind the bar, flash those beautiful eyes and that sexy body of yours at your guests, and be content with all the money you make."

"You are the biggest jerk I know, and I wouldn't accept your help if you begged me." She threw the rest of her beer at him.

Carson leapt from her seat and stormed to the exit. Ugh, the man was despicable and forced her to act crazy. Throwing a beer in his face was not her style. She needed to be the bigger person and apologize.

She took a look back, but he was being fawned over by Ms. Teenybopper Waitress. That ignited her anger even more, and any remorse she felt flew out the window.

Chapter 8

Carson squeezed her palms against her temples, hoping it would stop the drums pounding in her head. "That's it. No more drinking."

But it wasn't entirely her fault. After her little run-in with Hunter the night before, she stopped at the local BP gas station, bought a six-pack, and finished it. The thought of Hunter had her wondering if he had slept alone or entertained a certain too-young waitress.

"Who cares, Carson?" she yelled, causing her head to pound more.

She made her way to the bathroom. She ignored the numerous Post-it notes to check her complexion.

"Girl, you look like hell," she informed her reflection. Then she closed her eyes, twirled her finger a second, and placed it on today's affirmation.

With one eye open, she peered at the words she would recite the rest of the day, "You're destined for goodness."

She moved closer to the mirror, looking at her face from all angles while chanting her affirmation. If she kept this up, she'd look fifty before she was forty.

Before she could tear her gaze away from the mirror, she caught sight of the latest development, cringed, and immediately ceased chanting.

"Great, a new wrinkle. That wasn't there yesterday," she uttered in the empty bathroom.

Afraid she'd find more, she pulled herself away from the mirror, dragged herself into the shower, and turned the water to hot.

Twenty-five minutes later, she felt marginally better. She put on her robe and then went into the kitchen and microwaved a cup of yesterday's coffee, popped three Advils, made an egg-white omelet, and decided to get to work.

Her first order of business was to put a call into BJ. He wasn't at home, so she tried him at the office. He picked up after the first ring.

"Is that all you do, work?"

"My job's not exactly the typical nine to five, Carson."

"Jeez, someone woke up on the wrong side of the bed this morning."

She heard him sigh. "I'm sorry, Car. I just have a tough case I'm working on right now. What's up?"

"I hate to ask you this. I know you're busy. I need you to locate someone for me. Actually two people."

"Does this have to do with Emily?"

"Yes. The first person is someone she was real close to, and I don't believe he knows she's dead. I'd like to get in touch with him."

"Okay, what's his name?"

"Teddy. Well, I guess you need his real name Theodore Jackson II."

"I'll check with Biff at the country club and see if he's seen him." He laughed.

"Very funny. Can you do it?"

"Yeah, but I'm going to need a few days."

"Thanks."

"And the second person?"

"Maxim."

"Maxim what?"

"That's all I have, Maxim. And I think he lives in Franklin."

"Maxim in Franklin, that's not a lot to go on. What's this about?"

Carson told him about snooping around Emily's room and finding the letter.

"Good job, Detective. I'm impressed. You're sure you don't want to give up your bar job and come work for me?"

"No, thanks. After I solve Em's case, I'm giving up this PI business. It's more equipped for people like you."

"What's that supposed to mean?"

"Bye, BJ. Thanks." She smiled as she hung up the phone.

With the first order of business out of the way, it was time for her second task. She threw on a pair of sweatpants, her UT sweatshirt, and running shoes. A good long run should help to eliminate some of the toxins from her body.

The lake was more crowded than she thought it would be. The police tape no longer hung there to label it a crime scene. She chose a huge tree for leverage and began to stretch.

Pressing her right hand against the tree, her left hand grabbed her left ankle and pulled it behind her and against her butt. She tried to concentrate on the stretch, but her mind was filled with chatter as she watched the people moving all around her. A young couple strolled their baby; a man jogged by and gave her a smile. Then a few more guys ran by. Could one of those be Maxim? What if he was here right now enjoying a jog, knowing he got away with murder?

"Ouch." She pulled her hand from the bark to examine it. Her palm had a little nick from pressing too hard. Clearing all the clutter from her mind, she switched sides and stretched the right leg.

Two older ladies dressed in designer sweat suits, with huge rings on four of their fingers and rouged red cheeks, stopped at the tree next to hers. Carson gave them the partial "I don't know you, but I'm being a nice young girl" smile.

After a moment of eavesdropping, the smile disappeared.

"Such a shame, this beautiful lake has to be marred by the death of some drunk girl."

"I know. What is this world coming to? Used to be Brentwood was a safe, family-oriented community; and now, like all the other cities, it's being overtaken by hooligans."

"You ask me, that girl probably got what she deserved . . ."

"How dare you!" Carson advanced on the old ladies. "You gossiping old biddies." She ignored their gasps. "You have no idea what you're talking about. I'll have you know that the dead girl was murdered. What do you think about that? So your safe little town isn't being overtaken by hooligans, but by murderers!"

Both ladies looked at her as though she was crazy and took off without another word.

"Teach you to keep your opinions to yourselves," she yelled at their retreating backs.

Now that she had an adrenaline rush going, she decided to put it to use. She took off sprinting down the path where she had chased the little boy a few days ago.

After fifteen minutes and a stitch in her side, she gave up on running and decided to walk. Autumn had come, leaving most of the trees bare. For the first time, she noticed a few houses scattered along the hill. She knew of the ones on the road coming into the lake, but she hadn't known of these few buried in the woods. A picture of the cute blond boy popped into her mind, and she wondered if he lived in any of the houses.

Might as well put my new detective skills to work. There were two paths, one that she always took when she jogged around the lake and the other, much narrower, headed up into the woods. She opted for the newer trail. The path turned into less of a trail and more of a wild terrain the higher she climbed. She wondered what possessed people to live in such a remote area, how they got around, and if they had cable up this high.

Once she reached the first house, a couple of her questions were answered. She had climbed up the back side entrance to the little subdivision. Four houses sat in a little cul-de-sac. A road ran down the opposite side of the lake. And all this time she had thought there was only one entrance to the place.

Still somewhat winded from the climb, she took a few deep breaths before venturing up to the first house where she walked up the winding driveway.

She knocked on the door. Within a few minutes, a little old lady answered the door.

"Hello." Carson smiled. "I'm sorry to bother you, but I was looking for a little boy . . ."

"Oh dear." The older woman placed her white-and-blue-veined hand to her heart. "You've lost your little boy and in these woods. He wasn't snatched, was he? I hear that happens all the time these days. And then that little girl found dead last week. What's happening to our safe society? You can use my phone to call the police if you'd like."

"No, ma'am. I didn't lose a child. I'm looking for a little boy that I met at the lake the other day. He's got—"

"And he's not your son?"

"No, ma'am."

"What do you want with this boy who isn't your son?"

"Actually, I'm investigating the murder of that young girl from last week and—"

"Murder." She eyed Carson, suspiciously. "That girl's death was a drunken accident. Who are you?"

"My name's Carson O'Hara, and I happen to know the deceased. I can tell you it was no accident." She handed her a card.

"This card says you're a bartender."

"That's my side job." She knew it looked tacky, but she hadn't had time or thought to get new ones made that say PI.

"Now about that little boy, if you—"

"I don't know any little boy and don't bother me again." The elderly woman slammed the door with impressive force for someone with such a frail appearance.

"You have my card. Please call if you want to help." The only response was a click of the lock.

She headed to the next house.

The door was opened by Grizzly Adams. It took a minute for her to find her voice.

"Hi, I'm—"

"Whatever you're selling, I'm not interested," he growled.

"I'm not selling anything. I'm looking for a—" She was talking to a closed door.

No one answered the third house, so she pulled out one of her cards, wrote what and who she was looking for, then slipped it under the door.

She reached the last house and rang the bell. She swore she heard footsteps, so after a minute and no answer, she rang the bell again. Still there was no answer. That was odd because she heard steps. She stepped back and looked up at the house. A curtain moved. Someone was home, but why wouldn't they answer the door? She headed around the back of the house. Peering through the door window, she saw a half-eaten sandwich on the table. She tried the door, but it was locked. Grabbing a lawn chair, she placed it under the window and climbed up. The glass pane was open just a tad, and the screen was down. If she could just get the glass open a little more, she'd be able to pop open the screen. A trick she learned in her teens when she snuck out many a nights.

She just about had it.

"Freeze!"

Carson shifted too far to the right, which caused the chair to rock and then fell out from under her. She twisted and landed on her right arm.

"Don't move."

"Officer, there's been—" She was looking down the barrel of a gun.

Chapter 9

Carson rubbed the tips of her black, blue fingers against her sweatpants. It was no use the ink wasn't going away. It had been over an hour. Great, now she had a record, and she hadn't done anything wrong. Not really. It wasn't like she was truly breaking and entering. She only wanted to talk to the owners and find that little boy. Her tummy rumbled. She hadn't eaten that day and the headache she thought she erased, began to beat again.

"Dammit, dammit, dammit." She got off the hard wooden bench, her butt half asleep, and went to the jail cell door. Her hands gripped the bars as she pressed her face against the iron. She scanned the hallway. No one was around.

"Yoo-hoo, anybody. Hel-looo . . . Come on somebody. This has gone on long enough. I'm not a criminal." She spun around and leaned her back against the bars about to give up when she heard the jangle of keys.

"Finally, it's about time." She turned back around. "Hunter. What took you so long? I've been here for over an hour."

"It's been three hours." He looked bored.

"What? I've been in here for three hours. No wonder I'm hungry. Three hours. Could they not find you? Of course they couldn't find you or I won't have been here so long. I hope you set them straight."

"Oh, I set them straight all right. I'm the one who told them to keep you here."

"What?" Her right eyebrow rose up.

"I told you that if I found you playing detective I'd put you in a jail cell."

"Why you son-of-a . . ."

"Un, un, un." His index finger wiggled back and forth. "I am an officer, and I don't think you want to spend more time behind bars. Do you?"

Carson wanted to scream and punch him in his snug face. She always said anger made her ugly. She knew she must look like the wicked witch.

"This is about last night, isn't it?"

"This has nothing to do with last night."

"Right. This has nothing to do with your oversized ego and the fact that it got a little wet. Besides I'm sure miss pom-pom waitress helped soothe you after her shift."

A smile lit up Hunter's face. The audacity of the man.

"So you did sleep with her."

"Are you jealous?" his smile grew bigger.

"Pleazzz."

"I told you to stay away from police business and I meant it."

"Fine, point taken now am I free to go, off-icer." She hissed.

"That depends." He encircled his hands atop hers imprisoning them against the bar.

"Ugh." She tried to move her hands. It was no use. She didn't want to think about the warmth of his hand and the charge they set off through her body. The same hands that had caressed a certain waitress the night before. "You are a worm. A big, fat slimy one. Now get me out of here."

"Not until you tell me why you tried to break into someone's house, and what it has to do with Emily."

"It had nothing to do with Emily."

"Carson, I'm not playing games. Now tell me what you were doing."

"I . . . um was jogging through the hills and I thought I . . . uh, heard a scream.

"A scream?"

"Yep, that's right. I knocked on the door and no one answered. I saw a curtain move and someone peak out. So of course I got worried. I ran around the back, looked in the window. There was a half eaten sandwich on the table and a chair was overturned. So, I got even more worried that someone was in real trouble. That's when I tried to get in the window and then the friendly police shoved a gun in my face."

"God, you're something you know that?" He pulled his hands away from the bars and raked them through his hair. "That's your story."

"It's true." Except for the scream. He didn't need to know that.

"I don't think you ever told the truth since I met you."

The fact that he called her a liar stung a little big. "That's my story."

"And I'm supposed to believe this."

"Frankly, detective I don't care what you believe."

"I should leave you here all night."

"Does that mean I'm being charged with something, detective? Is the owner of the house pressing charges?" She hoped the fear in her belly didn't reflect in her eyes.

"No, Mrs. Berringer is not pressing charges." He breathed. "She wants to forget the whole thing happened. So," he unlocked the jail cell. "You're free to go."

"Thank you, detective." Carson passed through the door. Without a glance in his direction, she kept walking.

"Oh, Carson."

She stopped and looked over her shoulder.

"I will find out what the connection is between you, Mrs. Berringer and Emily. And then you and I will have a nice little sit down . . ."

She turned away and started walking.

"And . . . ." He raced over and grabbed her arm. " . . . If you are somehow obstructing justice in any way, you'll be in there." He nodded toward the jail cell. "A lot longer then three hours."

"Are you through threatening me, Detective?" She yanked her arm free.

"Ah, Carson."

She felt bars against her back. He somehow backed her against the wall.

"I'm not threatening you." He leaned down his nose touching hers. "I'm promising you. I think it's about time you took me a little more serious."

His breath was warm across her face. And the tone of his voice sent a shiver down her spine. Oh, god would he kiss her. She closed her eyes and suddenly felt alone. She opened them back up and he was gone.

A sigh of relief escaped her lips. She needed to find Emily's killer and fast. She wasn't sure how many more run-ins she'd survive with Hunter. If she were a betting woman, she bet not many.

*   *   *

"Here drink this." Jessie placed the hot mug of cocoa in Carson's hands.

She took a sip. "Um. A little more than just cocoa."

"A little peppermint schnapps to take the edge off. I can't believe he kept you in jail for three hours."

"I know." Carson took another sip. It's about time her best friend sided with her.

"You must have really made him mad."

"What?" Carson choked on her cocoa.

"It's just a little much. Hunter doesn't seem like that type of person."

"How would you know? You hardly know the man."

"I know that he cares about you."

"Right. That's why I spent three hours in jail."

"Suit yourself but I've never been wrong when it comes to you and men. And I saw the way he looked at you at Em's funeral. There is some definite sparks going on there."

"Well then Mrs. Know it all. How about this? Your so-called hero went home with a teeny-bopper waitress and slept with her. Explain that one." She took a smug gulp of her chocolate.

"No, not his style. Probably said it to make you jealous. And I say it worked."

Damn it. Why had she brought up the waitress? She showed her hand and now Jamie would never leave her alone about Hunter. "I give up. I can't even talk to my best friend."

"Hey, that's not fair?"

"Well, you are siding with the enemy."

"Carson, you know I support you in anything you do as long as it makes you happy. But you're not happy. And it's not just Emily. Something was missing in you before she died. But I'm worried about you and what you're getting yourself into. And I for one am glad that Hunter's around. At least I know someone's going to be there to take care of you. And that makes me sleep better."

"Gee Jamie . . ." Carson put her cup on the counter. "I didn't realize I was causing you to lose sleep." She hugged her.

"Now you know, but one thing that might stop me from worrying."

"I don't want to know."

"Marry Hunter."

"Ugh." She pulled away and swatted Jamie across the head.

"You have to admit. You'd make beautiful babies."

"That's it I'm out of here."

"Okay. I'll stop. Don't go. I rented this movie. It's due back tomorrow. I have a couple of hours before the baby's back from his grandmothers. Let's order a pizza, veg out and watch the movie."

"Okay. But Hunter's name is banned for the rest of the afternoon."

"Scouts honor. I'll order the pizza while you get the movie ready."

"Fine." She headed up the stairs. "I want extra cheese on my pizza." She yelled down.

It was after midnight when Carson returned home from her movie marathon at Jamie's. Her message light was blinking. She pressed play.

"Hey Car, its Jack-" Carson hit the erase button. When would the boy get it through his head that they were over?

She crawled into bed wanting to leave this horrendous day behind her. But sleep eluded her when each time she closed her eyes; images of Hunter making love to a waitress filled her mind. Especially since the waitress was her.

Chapter 10

His hands were soft and sure as they glided across her body. She breathed in his warm masculine scent. Her eyes fluttered open to be greeted by magnificent aquamarine ones.

"You don't know how long I've wanted to do this," his husky voice whispered.

"Oh yes, I do," her voice caught as his hand trailed up her rib cage. "I want you so much."

She heard a ringing sound. "What's that noise?"

"It's nothing." His lips hovered close to hers.

The ringing got louder as his lips got closer.

She opened her eyes to see his expression, wondering if he was as turned-on as she was; but instead of his gorgeous face, she was eyeing her bedroom ceiling. Carson sat up in bed and slammed the Off button on her alarm.

It was only a dream. Carson moaned as she fell back to her pillow. "Damn that man."

Thirty minutes later, dressed in her running clothes, she was out the door. The sun shone bright, but last night's storm had brought in a cold front. She inhaled a fresh gulp of air, loving that cool, crisp morning aroma that smelled like burning wood.

She stopped at Mickey Dee's, ordered three breakfast burritos with a large coffee to go. She grabbed her order, anxious to get to the lake.

It was Saturday. Recalling her childhood, she remembered how she liked to be up early in the morning so she could play all day. But kids today didn't play like that. Except for maybe one little boy with big green eyes and blond hair. And she hoped he felt like playing today.

She parked the car, grabbed her breakfast, and trotted toward the place where Emily had been murdered. As Carson got closer to the lake, she saw the place was a muddy mess. She looked down at her semiwhite tennis shoes now caked with muck. It was about time for a new pair anyway.

The mud squished beneath her shoes and crusted the sides as she made her way to the man-made bridge. She placed her breakfast on the rail then scraped her feet across the bridge to loosen some of the mud.

Eying the cooling burritos, she decided to forget about her ruined shoes. She took a bite, savoring the flavor of cheese, egg, sausage, and hot sauce. She was about to take another bite when she caught a flash of movement from the corner of her eye.

He sat on the edge of the bridge watching her.

She grabbed the bag. "I brought you some breakfast." She took a step toward him. He took a step back.

"Okay. I won't come any closer." She bent down, placed the bag on the wooden plank, then pushed it toward the towheaded boy. Then she stood back up and walked toward the other side of the bridge. Ignoring him, she finished her burrito and stuffed the wrapper into her pocket. What could she do to get close to the boy? He was afraid of his own shadow, but why? Yet she sensed he liked her and that he wanted to talk to her. Well, here she stood; all he had to do was speak. Maybe this boy was a dead end. She sighed then took a sip of her coffee.

A minute crawled by, then another. She took another swallow of her java. At this rate, she'd soon be drinking ice coffee. Not to mention the food, it probably tasted more like processed junk than normal. Instinct made her look over her shoulder. The bag was gone.

Panicking, she spun around and was about to give chase until she saw little feet dangling and kicking from a rock.

Slowly, she proceeded down the bridge. When he was in her line of vision, she stopped.

"My name's Carson, but my friends call me Car."

The boy looked up at her. Bits of sausage, egg, and cheese hung on his chin. "Car." He giggled then took another bite of his burrito.

She smiled. "I guess that name sounds silly, huh?" She inched closer.

"I like cars. I have whole bunch of 'em. My dad says it's the biggest bunch in the whole world." He stretched out his arms. "Want a see 'em?"

"Sure. I like cars too. In fact, I have a real cool car. It's a convertible."

"What's a conbertible?" He continued kicking his feet against the rock.

"It's a car whose top comes off. Maybe if your parents say it's okay, I'll give you a ride in it someday."

"Cool. I mean no, I can't do that."

"It would be fun."

"I'm not allowed to take rides from strangers."

"I understand. Why don't you show me some of your cars, and we can play with them."

"I guess . . ." He slid off the back side of the rock and tore through the trees.

Carson cursed herself for having scared him off. She'd been so close, only to blow it.

""Wait—"

"Who are you talking to?"

She whirled around, surprised to find Hunter behind her. "How long have you been standing here spying on me?" she accused. He had to have seen the boy. And she bet his question was a ploy to catch her in a lie.

"Whoa, I wasn't spying on you. I just walked up and heard you talking." He looked over her shoulder into the woods. "Anyone I know?"

"Myself," popped out of her mouth. "It's a bad habit of mine. I picked it up from my mother."

His gaze strayed from the woods and landed on her, a skeptical smirk on his face. "So you came to the lake for a little exercise and a nice, quiet conversation with yourself?"

"Funny." She curled her lips. "What are you doing here, and why are you sneaking up on people and scaring them to death?"

"Sorry, I didn't mean to scare you."

"Well, you did. What do you want?"

"I went by your house. After a couple of minutes of knocking, I knew you were probably avoiding me. I figured I'd find you here. I wanted to talk to you." He held out a cup of coffee.

"I already have a cup." She dangled it in front of him. "Now, good-bye."

"I wanted to apologize about yesterday."

"Apology not accepted." She moved past him but didn't get too far.

He used the hood of her sweatshirt to pull her back toward him. His smell was clean and outdoorsy, exactly as she dreamed it. She felt her cheeks burning as the dream came to full life in her mind. "Let go of my hood."

"Carson, I'm sorry about yesterday. I know I went a little overboard."

"A little. You were cruel and unacceptable."

"It was the only thing I could think of to keep you safe."

"Safe? I'm glad your idea of keeping me safe entails me spending hours in a jail cell. I know." She snapped her fingers. "Next time, why don't you send me to Tennessee Prison for Women in downtown Nashville? I could use some new friends."

"Listen, I'm sorry. But you left me no choice."

Her mouth fell open. The audacity of the man blaming this on her, he was the one who refused to believe Emily was murdered. If he'd help her, she wouldn't have to take such drastic measures.

"Oh, I left you plenty of choices. You just choose to be an unfeeling bully. Now, I'll ask you again. Let me go."

"Not until you accept my apology and promise to be good and talk to me."

"Fat chance." She tried to pull away.

He pulled her hood harder, bringing her back side against his chest. "All I want to do is talk." The whisper of his breath sent tiny beads of excitement through her veins as well as goose bumps across her flesh. She bit her lip, forcing her body not to shiver in his arms. *I don't like this man. He is the enemy*, she reminded herself. Maybe if she talked to him, he'd go away and her body would stop screaming sex. And how dare her body betray her after he left her to rot in a jail cell for three hours.

"Okay, we'll talk." She refused to acknowledge the burning in her belly.

It seemed an eternity passed before he released her. She turned to face him. The glassy look in his eyes let her know that he had been just as affected by their touch as she had. She almost smiled at the pained look in his eyes.

"Talk." She crossed her arms over her chest.

"I've decided to unofficially reopen Emily's case."

Her eyebrow arched. "What do you mean unofficially?"

"It means I'm doing it without the help of my department. I need more evidence to support your theory that she was murdered before I can go to my captain to get it opened."

Carson stared at him. "Why?"

"I can't get into the logistics of it. Why are you questioning me? I thought you'd be pleased."

"I guess it doesn't matter as long as it's getting done." She clapped her hands. "Where should we start?" She tapped her index finger against her lips. "I guess . . ." The rest of her words died on her lips as she caught Hunter shaking his head.

"What?"

"There's one stipulation."

"No, don't even say it."

"Carson, you have to stay out of it. I don't want you anywhere near or involved with this case."

"I'm not listening." She slapped her hands over her ears. "La, la, la, I can't hear you."

"Carson." He pulled her hands away from her ears.

"Your cruelty knows no bounds."

"I'm not doing this to be cruel. I'm doing this to protect you. It's a job for professionals."

"I don't need your protection."

He grabbed her by both arms and shook her. "Do you realize how dangerous this is? We are looking for a cold-blooded killer. One I believe that has no qualms about killing innocent people. In fact, I think this person enjoys killing, which makes them even more dangerous. I won't have you getting hurt or killed."

"And I won't have you keeping me in the dark."

"Dammit." He kicked the gravel and paced in a circle.

"Hunter." She placed her hand on his arm. "She was the closest thing I had to a sister. She didn't deserve to die like that. And I'm not going to let you pump me for information while I sit on the sidelines like a dog, hoping you'll throw me a bone. Either we do this together, or I do it alone."

"Carson, I can't take the chance."

"If you're around, nothing will happen to me. I was her closest friend. No one knows her like I do. You need me. Besides, I have some ex—, some good ideas." The words flew out of her mouth a mile a minute.

"Like breaking into innocent people's houses, or would those be the things you learned during your short stint in the police academy?"

Carson blanched. "How did you . . . you had me investigated?"

"It's a murder case. Everyone needs to be checked out."

"I'm a suspect?" She gritted her teeth. "You'd actually think I'd kill my good friend?"

He sighed. "I've seen worse, but no, I don't think that. Besides, I had you investigated right when I met you. So tell me about the academy."

Her head spun from the knowledge that Hunter had run a check on her. What else had he found out? Who was she kidding, he probably found out everything. But he'd just sit on it, and he'd wait for her to open up and reveal one of the most horrible events of her past. Never.

"It's in the past where it belongs." She needed to get away from here, but not until she made Hunter see she belonged on this case.

"I want to help find Emily's killer," she said, hoping to distract him from any further questions about her past.

"Carson, I'm not budging on this. It's my way or no way."

"Meaning?"

"Meaning, if you don't promise me right now to let me do this alone, I'll put you back in jail for obstruction of justice."

"You're bluffing." She looked at him, but his expression remained unchanged. Maybe he was serious. Dammit, she needed his help. "Hunter, listen—"

"Carson, your word."

"Hunter, you need me."

"What I need is to know that you're safe."

"I will be safe. Nothing's going to happen to me. Not with you around." And deep in her heart, she knew she spoke the truth.

"Carson, I can't do my job if I'm constantly worried about you."

"You won't even know I'm around."

"Oh, believe me, I'll know."

"Hunter."

"Carson, dammit. Your word or I swear I'll hog-tie you to the bed and leave you there until I find this killer."

Visions of Hunter tying her to the bed and having his way with her filled her senses. Carson groaned at how traitorous her mind and body have become where he was concerned. Minutes passed before she gained control of her senses.

"I promise." With her fingers crossed, she gave him her best pouty face.

"Good." His voice was full of relief. "There's one more thing I want to discuss with you."

"Hunter, I don't want to discuss—"

"Have dinner with me tonight."

Her eyes clashed with his. "Dinner, tonight?" The thought of it sent a warm feeling to her midsection. He wanted to have dinner with her.

Who was she kidding? She couldn't believe she was even contemplating the idea. There was no way. The two of them just didn't go together. He was a cop. And like other cops, she knew he'd use his authority to bully and get his way. That's exactly what he was doing now. There was no way she'd go down that path once again.

Didn't the guy leave her in a jail cell the day before?

But the wonderful image of him above her in her bed flashed in her mind. Jessie conversation about how beautiful their baby would be played in her brain. She tripped over her feet.

Hunter caught her. His strong hands encircled her waist. "Are you okay?"

The dream grew more vivid in her mind. His right hand held on to her arm while his left held the small of her back. She felt the warmth of his touch right through her sweatshirt.

She backed away. "I can't make it tonight. So I'll see ya." She started to walk away.

"Then how about tomorrow night?"

She stopped and placed her hands in her pocket. "I'm not looking to get involved with anyone right now."

"It's just dinner."

Just dinner, huh, how many women had he said that to? It could never be just dinner to her, and she couldn't just be another in a long list of dinners. Rationally, she knew he was out of bounds, but her body's reaction to him was anything but rational. She feared where Hunter was concerned, resistance was futile.

But she knew this man could hurt her, and she wasn't willing to take the chance.

"Thanks but no thanks." She turned to leave.

"Who are you afraid of—me or you?"

Both of us. "I'm not afraid of anything," she called over her shoulder.

"Then prove it," he dared.

"Nice try, but it's not going to work."

"Well, what does work with you? I can't scare you or dare you. You're a pain in the ass. You know that?"

"Bye, Hunter." She waited until she was out of his view before she sprinted to her car.

Halfway home, she remembered her reason for being at the lake. She'd been so close to befriending that little boy and finding out his name. Then he got one look at Hunter and bolted like a rabbit.

What made such a young boy so afraid of people? Or was his fear only for men? Maybe it was better to keep the boy a secret, for now. Getting Hunter involved could scare the boy away for good. That was one thing she couldn't afford. He was involved somehow; she just knew it.

Bits of her miniscule conversation with the little boy played in her head. He mentioned his father liked cars. Did that mean he lived with Grizzly Adams? Or in the house she almost broke into. And maybe he didn't live up there at all. Was it a habit for him to be roaming the woods? And if so, did he see Em the night she died?

The unanswered questions that swirled in her mind turned into a pounding headache by the time she reached home. She just wasn't cut out for this PI business.

The one good thing that happened that morning was Hunter was going to reopen the case, and whether he liked it or not, she was going to help him.

Chapter 11

As soon as Carson entered her apartment, she headed to the kitchen. She picked through the vegetable bin until she found a fresh lime then sliced it in half and rubbed it against her forehead. Within minutes, the throbbing began to subside. It was an old remedy she had discovered during her holistic healing phase. She didn't know if it was all psychological, but as long as it worked, she didn't care. She hated taking any type of medication.

She ignored the blinking answering machine, opting for a nap. After some minutes, she found herself staring at the ceiling. She pressed the crook of her elbow across her eyes to block the sun. Maybe that would help her sleep. But she knew that wasn't the problem. Her problem was one Hunter Reeves. The man was as unpredictable as a hurricane. Even though he decided to help her in Em's case, something about it niggled at the back of her mind. She just couldn't put her finger on it. And he found out about her stint at the academy. How could he? It was so long ago; she was just an inexperienced girl. She didn't know, but weren't those things sealed and kept quiet? A sighed escaped her lips. Just goes to show that cops stick together no matter how bad some cops can be. This wasn't going to work. Carson swung her legs to the floor and pushed herself off the couch.

Curiosity got the better of her. She went back to the living area and played her message.

The first one was from her mother, telling her she was forgiven for her behavior. The second message was from her father, informing her she was in his doghouse for letting her mother come home. Parents, she rolled her eyes, they can be such children at times.

Her ears perked up at the third message. It was from BJ. He wanted her to call him. She didn't hesitate picking up the phone. He answered on the second ring.

"Hey, BJ, it's Carson. Guess what?" She didn't give him a chance to speak. "Hunter decided to reopen Em's case."

"Really. Wow."

"Um, BJ, I'm not sure that was the response I was expecting. This is great news." Suspicion wiggled at the back of her mind.

"Yeah. Car, did he say why?"

"I didn't ask him why. What does it matter why?" But for some reason, she knew it mattered.

"It's nothing."

"BJ? What is it?"

"It doesn't make sense. Why the sudden change of heart? It's not like Hunter to second-guess himself and change his mind."

Carson twirled the phone's cord around her finger. "Maybe I had enough evidence to convince him."

"Yeah. Umh . . . sure . . . You know, you're probably right."

"BJ," she warned.

"Well, the guy's adamant about closing the case, then he's kissing you; and next thing you know, he's reopening the case. You know what, forget it. I'm sure I'm being stupid. You know you're probably right. You can be pretty convincing at times." He laughed.

It didn't work. Carson's heart dropped to her stomach. No, she was the stupid one. He said it was unofficial—that only he was working on it. Not even a minute later, he was asking her out to dinner. Deep down she knew it was too good to be true.

"Carson, are you there?"

BJ's voice stifled her thoughts. "I'm here."

"I said how did you convince Hunter to help you?"

She didn't. She wanted to scream. He was just using Em's death for his own selfish purpose. No, he couldn't be that much of a cad. But damn it, he was a cop, and she knew firsthand how ruthless they could be. She couldn't believe that. Not even Hunter could be that methodical and cruel. Yet he did let her stew in jail for three hours.

"He didn't say."

"Car, talk to me. What's going on?"

"Do you have that information for me?"

"Well, half of it. I found Theodore, but Maxim is still a mystery. Can you give me anything else about the guy?

"No, I'm sorry I can't."

"Okay, do you have a pen and paper?"

She grabbed a pen and a paper napkin. "I'm ready."

Carson hung up the phone with BJ and then punched in Hunter's number. She called the station. "Detective Reeves, please."

He answered within seconds. "Detective Reeves here."

"Detective."

"Carson, what a nice surprise. Have you changed your mind about dinner?"

She could picture his lazy triumphant grin. "Not quite. In fact, I wouldn't go out to dinner with you if you were the last man on earth. You self-serving ass."

"Whoa, what's gotten into you?"

"You and your games, acting like the big hero, so concerned about Emily's case, knowing it was just a ploy. What were you hoping for? That'd I'd be so grateful I'd just fall into bed with you? You're pathetic. I should call your captain and have you brought up on charges or something."

"Carson . . ."

"You had no intention of reopening this case."

"I have every intention. In fact, I was working on something right now."

"God, you must really think I'm stupid. I'm sure you and your cop buddies are just laughing away at how easily you played me for a fool."

"Carson, it's not like that."

"Save it. I'm not a stupid bimbo taken in by your charm." She slammed down the receiver. Carson wasn't sure what she expected from the phone call to Hunter, but it wasn't to feel worse, which she did.

There wasn't any time to dwell on Hunter and his scheming ways. She had other business to take care of.

She looked down at the napkin with Teddy's number on it. To tell him over the phone would be too impersonal. She needed to see him in person. He lived in Johnson City. That wasn't too far. She had the rest of the day and tomorrow off. Carson could use a little trip.

One night bag and forty minutes later, Carson was driving down Highway 44 toward Knoxville. It was another gorgeous day. No clouds littered the azure blue sky. Some of the trees still hung on to their orange-burnt leaves, but most were stripped bare. The only thing that marred the beauty of the drive was the road construction, which caused stop-and-go traffic. She couldn't remember the last time there wasn't some type of work being done to Tennessee's roads.

Tired of driving with her foot on the brake, Carson contemplated Lebanon's Prime Outlet Shops as it loomed into view. It wouldn't hurt to browse a little bit. By that time, maybe some of the slow traffic would subside. Driving around the back side of the mall, she parked the car. She walked to the map and devised a plan of action. She'd hit Polo, Liz Claiborne, and Nike then maybe mosey on into Gap. But she'd buy nothing. This was strictly browsing time and a way to get that louse Hunter Reeves out of her head.

An hour, three bags, and a couple of credit card receipts later, Carson was back in her car. How was she supposed to know the stores were having an incredible sidewalk sale? She'd never know when she'd find deals that good again.

At least some good came out of her plan. The traffic wasn't as heavy, and she was able to drive sixty down the road.

Carson reached the little town a little after five in the afternoon. She pulled into the gas station. Pulling out her map, she found Teddy's street and traced her way to his house. She parked across the street. His block was quaint and cozy. She expected to see the Cleavers emerge from any one of the little A-frame homes. It amazed her how some towns stayed untouched, almost suspended in time. These people most likely left their doors unlocked at night.

It was Saturday night. She hadn't called Teddy to let him know she was coming. Something told her that if she had, he would have refused to see her. Carson prayed he was home. If he wasn't, she'd just spend the night and catch him in the morning. Either way, she'd see him.

She knocked on the door and waited; and within seconds, the door was answered.

"Hi, Teddy."

"Carson?" he croaked. "What are you doing here?" He looked behind her.

"I wanted to get away for the weekend. Ended up here, and I remembered someone told me you lived here. So I thought I'd look you up. For old time's sake." Wow, Carson couldn't believe the way he looked. He was well over six three. In high school, he'd been muscular with some fat around the middle, which earned him the nickname Teddy. He had been as cuddly as one. Now the fat was gone, and the bulky muscle was leaner and more defined. Yet there was a weary, cautious glint in his eyes.

"Teddy, you look great."

"As do you, but then again you always did."

If it had been anyone else but Teddy handing her the compliment, she might have blushed. He was always like a big brother to her. "Can I come in?"

"Sure." He ushered her into the house. "Can I get you something to drink?"

"Water would be great." Her mouth suddenly felt too dry. have a seat." He showed her into the family room. "I'll be right back with that water."

Carson took in the comfy surroundings and knew a woman had left her mark. Had it been Emily? Were they somehow connected again? The thought made her leap from her chair and make a beeline for the fireplace mantel where several pictures were lined. Did he keep any pictures of Emily, she wondered. She skimmed past the family pictures and focused on one. There was a picture of Teddy with his arm wrapped around a beautiful redhead. They both glowed. Hope dissipated, so much for thinking Teddy had been involved with Emily.

"That's my fiancée."

Carson knocked the picture over. How did he sneak up on her? "I'm sorry." She stood it back up and turned to face Teddy. "That's wonderful. She's very beautiful."

"Yes, she is. Here's your water." He handed her the glass.

"So when's the big day?" She took a sip.

"This coming spring."

"Congratulations."

"Thanks. Have a seat. Tell me what's been going on with you." He dropped into the recliner.

Carson sat opposite him on the love seat. Placing her water on the glass coffee table, she rubbed her hands down her thighs. "You're probably wondering what I'm doing here. Just showing up like this after ten years."

"I know why you're here." He looked grim.

"You do?"

He nodded. Was that a tear in his eye?

"My mother told me. She's still close to Mrs. Johnson. I'm sorry I haven't tried to contact you. I just—"

"But I didn't see you at the funeral."

"I know. I was out of town. I just got the message. My mother waited until I got home. She didn't want to spoil my trip."

"Gosh, I'm sorry I wasted your time."

"Nonsense, seeing a good friend is never wasted time. I'm glad you came."

"Thank you."

"No, thank you for being considerate enough to drive all this way to tell me about Emily. You're a true friend."

This time Carson did blush at the compliment. The rumble of Carson's belly disrupted the moment of awkward silence.

Carson pressed her hand against her stomach. "I haven't eaten since breakfast."

"Well, let's get you something to eat." Teddy laughed.

Carson smiled back. "I did notice a steak house when I drove in. Come on, I'll treat you and your beautiful bride-to-be to dinner."

"Sorry, you'll have to settle with only me. She's on a business trip."

"Let's go." She popped off the couch. "I'll drive."

"Yes, ma'am." He saluted. "Let me get my coat."

Five minutes later, they were seated in a corner booth.

"Is this place any good?" Carson opened her menu.

"Not bad. Besides the fact it's the only real restaurant in town. They make a great fillet."

"Sounds good to me." Carson closed her menu. The waiter came to the table, and Teddy ordered two fillets with baked potatoes, salads, and two draft beers.

"I like the décor in here, it's different." She looked all around. The place resembled an old horse stable. The floor was covered in hay, and the tables were in stalls. Which gave it an intimate feel.

"Carson."

She flinched at the feel of Teddy's hand atop hers.

He must have felt it because he snatched it back.

"Car, it's really good to see you."

"You too." She smiled.

"I'm still in a state of shock. I wished I could have been here for Emily, for Mrs. J, for you. It seems so surreal." He closed his eyes.

"I know." This time she placed her hand atop his. "It really sucks."

He opened his eyes and stared at her. "Is there anything I can do to help you to cope with this?"

"Thanks and no. I can't say it gets easier with time because it doesn't. But I find that if I remember the good times, I can keep her with me. And once I find her killer, I might be able to have some closure."

"Killer?" He looked around.

"Killer . . ." he repeated in a whisper. "Carson, what the hell are you talking about?"

The waiter brought their salads. Carson waited until he left then leaned across the table.

"Emily was murdered."

"Whoa." Teddy shook his head. "My mother told me she drowned. She didn't say anything about murder."

"C'mon, you know what a wonderful swimmer she was. She didn't drown. How many summers did we spend at that lake? And not just all of us, I know it was yours and Em's special place."

Teddy blushed and took another sip of his beer.

Carson smiled. "Don't worry, she only told me."

Teddy's expression turned serious. "Carson, if the cops said she drowned—"

"She was murdered. In fact, I have a cop looking into it." She didn't know if that was true any longer now that she was onto Hunter's game. He might not be aiding her. But saying it out loud made her feel better.

"What makes you think she was murdered?"

She shrugged her shoulder. "My gut tells me she was."

"Wait a minute. Your gut feeling. What the hell are you up to?"

Carson sat back, stunned by his sudden outburst.

"Carson, you pulled some crazy stunts in high school, but you've crossed the line this time."

"Teddy."

"God, she was your best friend and my first love. And you want to what? Turn her death into a circus just to appease some sense of your warped ideas."

"I don't know what you're talking about."

"Don't you. I knew you were jealous of her, but I never knew you had an evil streak."

"What are you talking about?"

"Oh, come on, Carson. There's some twisted part inside you that's glad Emily's dead."

"My god. How, how could you say that?" Her hand clutched her shirt.

Teddy looked as stunned as Carson did. Then a tear slid down his face. "Carson, I'm sorry I didn't mean it. But listen to what you're saying. Can you imagine anyone hating her enough to kill her? It's impossible."

"Teddy, that's just it. I don't think that. I think whoever killed her loved her too much." She held up a hand. "Before you rip into me again, I'm going on more than a hunch. I have proof."

Teddy shook his head. "Proof."

Their dinner arrived.

"Carson."

"Teddy, let's eat." But that was the last thing Carson wanted to do. She moved the food around her plate, taking only a few bites. Like two strangers on a bad blind date, they spent the next thirty minutes in silence.

The waiter cleared their plates, and they both declined coffee.

"Carson, tell my about this proof."

The waiter returned with their check.

"I'll tell you on the way home." Carson paid the bill. As they drove to Teddy's house, Carson told Teddy how Emily secretly came home and hid from everyone. She told him about the precious blond boy she discovered and about the mysterious love letter she found in Emily's bedroom addressed the week she died.

When she finished talking, she placed the car in park, letting Teddy absorb everything she told him.

After what seemed an eternity, he turned to her with an odd expression on his face. "Jeez, Carson, I don't know what to say, what to think. If what you say is true."

"It's true. I know it in my heart."

"Son-of-a-bitch." Teddy slammed his fist against the window, causing it to rattle. "She must have been so scared, so all alone."

"I've thought the same things myself."

"There's no way the person who did this loved her. I know what it feels like to love Emily. And there's no way someone that truly loved her could kill her. The person who did this is nothing but a cold-blooded killer."

They looked at each other; then Teddy asked, "Why don't you stay the night? I have plenty of room."

"Thanks, but I got a room at the hotel. Besides, I don't want to cause you any trouble. I believe you have concerned neighbors." She smiled at the silhouette peering through his next-door neighbor's curtains.

"It was good seeing you, Carson, and I'm truly sorry about what I said. I didn't mean it. I know how much you loved Emily." He got out of the car.

"I know you didn't mean it. This has been hard on everyone. I'm glad we got to see each other. I just wish it was under better circumstances. Take care of yourself and congrats once again on your engagement."

Teddy shut the car door then leaned through the window, his eyes dark and unreadable. "Carson, do me a favor and be careful. If what you say is true and Emily did know her killer, then there might be a good chance he knows you too and vice versa. And if there's anything I can do, please call." He tapped the window and turned away.

"Teddy, wait."

He came back to the car, bent down, and peered in the window. "Change your mind about the hotel?"

"No, actually, I forgot something. The love letter was signed with the initial M. Does that mean anything to you?" Why had she chosen not to tell him the name Maxim? She searched his face for recognition of the name. Nothing. She definitely needed to stop hanging around Hunter before she became too cynical and untrusting. This was Teddy; to even think he had a hand in Em's murder was ridiculous.

"M." He cleared his throat. "No, I couldn't help you there. Like I said, I haven't seen Em in a long time. Good night, Carson."

She watched him walk up the sidewalk. He reached the door, turned back again, and just looked at her. A forlorn expression tightened his features. A sudden chill swept through her. What if Teddy was right and she already knew Emily's killer. For the first time, she wasn't so sure she wanted to find the answers she craved.

Chapter 12

Exhaustion seeped into every pore of Carson's body. After she left Teddy's house, she bypassed the hotel and headed out of town. Teddy's words still haunted her. He had been so angry at her, actually accused her of being happy that Emily was dead. She didn't know if she'd ever be able to forget the hate in his eyes or forgive him for his harsh words. She just knew she wanted to get as far away from him and be home. So she kept driving. Halfway home, she pulled over to a rest area for a power nap. The thirty-minute luxury hindered more than it helped. She spent the rest of the ride home with the top down, hoping the cold air would keep her awake. And it worked.

Rubbing the grit from her eyes, she focused on the lock and let herself into the apartment. Bed, that's all she needed. She walked down the hallway, opting not to turn on the lights. That was too much work. She had reached the love seat when the light flicked on.

"Where have you been?"

She screeched then took her overnight bag and knocked Hunter in the head. Carson pulled back to swing again; but Hunter ducked under the bag, came up, grabbed her around the waist, pinning her to the floor.

Panting, she attempted to kick out, but Hunter was too strong. "Get off me." She squirmed.

"Do you promise to stop hitting?"

"Yes."

Hunter got up and offered his hand. Ignoring it, Carson rolled to her side and pushed herself up. "How did you get into my apartment?"

"You'd be surprised by the power of the badge."

"Now that you scared ten years off my life, you can leave."

"Not until I set the record straight and convince you I'm not on this case to get you into bed."

"Really, then explain why you opened the case unofficially and, not two seconds later, you asked me out to dinner?"

"It's complicated." He ran a hand through his hair and remained silent.

Her adrenaline subsided, leaving her wearier than before. "I thought so. Just get out." She waved.

Hunter steadied her then took a deep breath. "My partner was killed six months ago. It was a very controversial case. There's been a lot of scrutiny and investigation into our precinct. I was told to be a 100 percent sure on Emily's case. And I was until I met you. So if I went to my captain now with no real hard evidence, I know he won't reopen it, and he'd make sure I didn't either. That's why I'm doing this on my own." He rubbed his left hand down his face. "I can't believe I'm telling you this."

Carson heard the sadness in Hunter's voice as he mentioned his dead partner. Obviously, he cared a great deal about the man. Carson wanted to take him in her arms and soothe his pain the way he'd done the night she'd found out about Emily.

"I'm—"

"Let me finish." Hunter held up his hand. "As for asking you out, you can deny it all you want, but there is something between us. God knows I don't want there to be. You are the last thing I need in my life. Nothing but trouble, but I can't seem to get you out of my head. Maybe if we stop denying it, we can make something happen and get on with our lives." He took a step toward her.

Great, the man thinks one night of sex can fix everything. Men. "Just when I think I could like you, you open your mouth."

He laughed right before he grabbed her and pulled her toward him. His mouth settled over hers. Carson's stomach dropped, and her toes curled up. A spark ignited inside her, melting the weariness from her bones. She felt every muscle of his hard body pressed against hers. Even though she'd never seen him naked, she knew he had a beautiful body. Her arms wound around his neck. She blamed her response on lack of sleep. What else could it be?

His lips never left hers as he propelled her toward the bedroom. Within seconds, the back of her legs came up against the bed. She fell across it, bringing Hunter with her. His kiss became urgent; then he tore his mouth away from hers. She moaned, wanting more. Much, much more.

"Don't go anywhere, I'll be right back." He left the room.

Carson draped her arm across her eyes, reality setting in. What was it he had said? "Let's just get together so we could both go on with our lives." That'd be just fine for Hunter. He might be able to turn it on and off with any woman, but she knew that once she let Hunter into her bed, her life would never be the same.

This had to stop before she did something stupid, like fall in love with the big jerk. The sound of him rummaging through the bathroom faded out as her body began to shut down.

The bed dipped, warning her that he was back. Wrapping his arm around her, he nuzzled her neck. "Carson."

"Mmmmmh." She curled into a ball.

"Carson."

She closed her eyes tighter and feigned sleep. It was the only course of action she could take.

"Car?"

She played dead as he shook her.

"God, woman, you are killing me."

The bed shifted, letting her know he had gotten up. She felt him tuck the blanket around her, his lips brushed her forehead, and then she heard the click of a closing door.

Carson rolled to the right side, hugging her pillow. Opening her eyes, she read the clock. It was one o'clock. She pulled the blanket over her head. The blanket Hunter had put over top of her. What a sweet gesture! Jack would never have thought to do that. He'd have been so mad that he didn't get laid that he'd have left her to freeze. No, she had to stop this. There was no way she could let Hunter become a hero; it would be the end of her. Like a child burning with fever, she threw the blanket to the ground and got out of bed.

Coffee. Strong black coffee was what she needed. She trudged into the kitchen. There was a note attached to the coffeepot. "Dinner. Tonight. I'll pick you up at eight."

A smile touched her lips. It dissolved into a frown. Smiling, she was actually smiling about having dinner with Hunter. Last night had been too close a call. The two of them couldn't have a relationship.

The phone rang. "Hello," she answered.

"Hi, sweetie."

"Abby. What are you doing? How's New Orleans treating you?"

"Not as friendly as I'd like."

"I miss you too." Carson laughed.

"I figured as much. That's why you need to get your ass down to Bleacher's this minute."

"What, you're here? Why didn't you call me?"

"Isn't that what I'm doing? Besides, I left a gazillion messages yesterday."

Carson glanced at the blinking machine. She'd been too preoccupied last night to check her messages. "I'll be there in half an hour." She hung up.

Dressed in faded blue jeans and a New York Giant's sweater, Carson entered the smoky, overcrowded sports bar. The wide screen displayed the Packers/Viking's game. A large group sat in front, dressed in yellow-and-green Packer colors, and right behind them sat a group of purple-and-gold Vikings fans. Cheers erupted as Packers intercepted the ball, ran it back for a touchdown, taking the lead. Carson smiled as the two tables started taunting each other. Nothing beats the thrill of watching Sunday afternoon football in a sports bar.

She headed left toward the back room where Abby sat at their favorite table.

"Carson," she squealed as she jumped up from her chair.

The two women embraced as if it'd been fifteen years between visits, not six months. Abby pulled her down into the booth and grabbed a beer out of the bucket of ice that sat on the middle of the table. "Here." She handed it to Carson. "Girl, what is with the dark circles? Busy last night, is that why you didn't call me back?"

"No." Carson wanted to laugh at the devilish glint in Abby's eyes. "I went out to Johnson City for the day and got home late." Deciding to forgo any mention of Hunter's visit, she sipped her beer. When it came to her love life, Abby was just as bad as Jamie. She didn't need two of her friends pushing Hunter down her throat.

"Johnson City, ugh. Why would you want to waste a perfectly good Saturday in that town?"

"Oh, excuse me. What? Now that you live in the fast-paced, exotic New Orleans, the little quaint family towns aren't good enough."

"Yeah," they responded in unison.

"Seriously." Abby reached out her hand, and Carson grabbed it. "I'm so sorry about Emily. We were never that close, but I know how much she meant to you. Why didn't you call me? I would have come in a heartbeat."

Carson's smile faded. The dinging of an electronic dartboard sounded in the background, indicating someone had just won a game of darts.

"Like you said . . . you weren't that close. Besides, you can't just drop everything and come babysit me. Speaking of your life It was time for her to change the subject. "You've been down in the Big Easy for six months, when are you going to make an honest man of Gary."

"As soon as I can whip him into shape." Once again they both laughed, the serious conversation was better left forgotten.

"So how long are you in town for?"

"It depends. How long can I stay at your place?" Abby popped open her second beer.

"As long as you want." Carson put her beer down. "Is everything okay?"

"Yes. Gary is almost finished with culinary school, but he has the opportunity to spend the next eight weeks in Paris working with a top chef. And of course, I can't afford to go. So—"

"That's great. I'd love to have you."

Abby raised her beer. "Here's to great friends." They clinked their glasses together before she added, "Old and new and, from what I understand, very sexy."

Carson set her beer down. "You spent last night at Jamie's, didn't you?" Great, just what she needed. Now she'd have two friends on her case about Hunter. She picked her beer back up and took a big swig.

Abby shrugged. "Oh, Carson, come on. I heard he was hot. The sexiest thing since Mel Gibson in *Mad Max*. I want to hear all about this Hunter guy."

"There's nothing to tell."

"That's not what I heard. I heard he has the hots for you."

"End of discussion," Carson said.

"Jeez, when did you become such a party pooper?"

"I don't know. When did you become such a nosy body?"

"Fine, I'll drop it for now. So tell me about being a PI. It sounds exciting."

Carson rolled her eyes. "Jamie didn't leave anything out, did she?"

They spent the next half hour discussing Carson's PI skills or lack thereof. The rest of the time, they caught up on the past six months, reminisced, and pigged out on greasy cheese fries and burgers.

The last beer pushed Carson over the edge. All she wanted to do was go home. She glanced at her watch. It was only seven thirty. Thirty minutes until Hunter would show up at her empty house. There was no way she could go to her apartment, but she didn't want to stay at the bar anymore. Not to mention, neither one of them could drive. Just then Jamie arrived at the table.

"Jamie, what are you doing here?"

"I called her," Abby answered. "Figured we could use the ride."

"C'mon, party girls, let's go. I'll take you to Carson's house."

"No. We can't." Carson jumped up. "Ants."

"Ants?" Abby curled her lip.

"Yeah. I've been having a real problem with them. So I used one of those debugger thingamajigs and it lasts for"—she tried to calculate the time in her fuzzy mind—"oh, seven hours."

"Seven hours!" Abby glanced at her watch. "How long has it been?"

"We still have another hour and a half." Carson tilted her head to the left.

"What are we supposed to do? I sure don't want to stay here anymore."

"We could hang out at Jamie's."

"No. My house is a mess. The baby's sick, and Tom's not too happy that I left him with his crying son."

"That's a man for you." Abby hiccupped.

"Tom happens to be a great father." Jamie crossed her arms over her chest.

"No one said he wasn't," Carson interjected.

"I know." Abby snapped her fingers. "We'll go to the lake and help Carson with her PI work. Maybe we'll find something she missed."

Carson noticed Jamie's eyes light up. Carson quickly cut in. "I doubt we'd find anything, besides, it's getting dark."

"I heard perps like to return to the scene of the crime," Abby said.

"Perps. Girlfriend, you're watching too much Discovery Channel." Carson shook her head.

"Then I say we go back to Car's house and deal with ant debugger smell."

"Okay, we'll go to the lake," Carson relented. She could use a fresh pair of eyes. And with no one around, maybe they'd find something the police missed. Besides, the three of them visiting the scene of a murder in the dark was safer than being alone on a date with Hunter.

Chapter 13

The pitch-black snakelike road forced Jamie to put on her high beams. Carson rubbed her arms to ward off the sudden chill that penetrated her body. What had Emily been thinking? How could she have come here willingly? For that matter, what the hell were they doing here? This park she loved by the light of the day seemed tainted at night and reeked of death and evil. Her chill increased as they came to the barrier.

Jamie stopped the car. "What do we do now? It says closed and only residents can go through."

Carson didn't miss the quiver in Jamie's voice. "I guess we need to leave." Great, now she'd have to face Hunter; but as she peered out into the darkness, it no longer seemed like a bad idea.

"How do they know we're not residents?" Abby added.

"They probably have stickers or something," said Jamie.

"I don't think it's going to matter because I doubt anyone is here," Abby fired back.

"But . . ." Jamie gripped the steering wheel.

"But nothing, Jamie, you were just as eager as I was to do this twenty minutes ago. Now stop being a chicken." Abby accused.

"Fine." Jamie put the car in gear and drove ahead.

"Stop here," Carson cried. Jamie stopped the car in front of a graveled road that was gated and padlocked. "This is where they found her."

"It's locked," said Jamie. "We'll have to come back during the day."

"What? The gate is all of four inches off the ground. All we have to do is climb over it." Abby opened the car door.

Jamie stared back at Carson. She shrugged her shoulders.

"C'mon, guys." Abby was out of the car.

"It's so dark out there," Jamie whispered.

Abby looked in through the window. "That's why we brought flashlights. Now, let's go."

Carson felt Jamie's fear. She didn't want to do this either, but something pulled at her, told her she needed to go out there and search. She climbed out of the backseat.

"Carson, I can't. It seemed like a great idea at the bar, but now—"

Carson looked back. Jamie's coloring had dropped two notches. "Don't worry. Stay here and lock the doors. We won't be long."

"What's taking you guys so long?" Abby called from the other side of the gate.

"Jamie's going to stay here and keep an eye on the car."

Abby turned, blasting her flashlight on Jamie. "Fine. Let's go, Carson."

Carson dragged her feet toward the gate as her eyes adjusted to the darkness. She hitched one leg over the metal rail then the other. The barren tree limbs reached out across the path in greeting. Clouds littered the dark sky, keeping the moon from lighting a path. The crunching gravel echoed through the cool, still air. She reached Abby about the same time that an owl screeched in warning.

Abby screamed as she collided with Carson, and they both crumbled to the cold, hard ground. For a few minutes, arms and legs flailed as they tried to disentangle themselves from each other.

"Carson, will you stop kicking me."

"I will when you get off me."

"Dammit. What was Emily thinking coming here alone?" Abby pushed Carson's leg off her stomach.

Carson stood up then helped Abby to her feet. "She was thinking that she trusted the person she was with."

Abby stopped brushing the dirt from her backside. "What do you mean?"

"She knew the person who killed her."

"How do you know that?"

"Because I found this love letter written to her the week she died. I don't care how much Emily had to drink, she'd never come here in the middle of the night. She was afraid of the—"

"Oh . . . my . . . god."

"What? What's the matter?"

"I forgot that Em was afraid of the dark. There's no way she would have come here alone. Look around you. This place is scary as hell. No one in their right mind would come here alone at night." Her mind conjured up the little blond boy. Would he really walk these woods alone at night? Carson scanned the blackened lake that claimed Em's life.

"Just look at us. We're basket cases while Jamie is locked in her car, scared to death."

"Do you want to go back?" Abby asked.

"Not yet. There's got to be something that can prove Em was murdered, something the police missed." Hunter flashed into her mind. She no longer needed to prove anything because he was going to help her. He believed her. She could mess up everything by being back here, but she couldn't let go. Turning this whole case over to Hunter and wiping her hands off it just left her feeling empty. The reality hit her full force. This wasn't only about helping Emily, it was about helping herself. For the first time in a long time, she finally had a sense of purpose.

"Gosh, Car, I wanted to come out here as kind of a joke, but you're taking this really serious."

"You're damn right I am. One of my best friends was murdered, and I'm going to find the bastard and . . . What do you mean a joke?" She let out a jagged breath, dropping her head back to relieve the tension that riddled her neck and shoulders.

"I just meant . . ."

"I know what you meant." She rolled her head to the right then to the middle and stared at Abby. "You're just like all the rest. You think I'm crazy, that I'm chasing an invisible killer, that Em drowned herself. Oh, Abby, I thought I could count on you to believe me."

Abby placed a hand on Carson's arm.

Carson shrugged it off. "Just go back to the car and sit with Jamie." She turned away.

"Carson, wait." Abby grabbed her arm. "You're right, I'm sorry. If you say Emily was murdered, then I believe you. And I'll help you look for whatever you think you'll find out here."

Carson took a deep breath. "Thank you. Let's stay close together, and we'll check over by the water."

Carson walked toward the water's entrance using the flashlight to guide her way. The lack of crickets chirping and frogs croaking along with the pitch-black of night left her feeling as though she were in the throes of death. A sudden breeze blew off the water, lifting the hair from her face.

Carson. The wind howled her name. She shook her head. *Carson.*

"Abby, stop that."

"Stop what?"

"Cute, I'm not playing games with you."

"What the hell are you talking about?"

Carson watched Abby's light bounce through the brush a foot from her, and in the opposite direction, Abby's flashlight beam moved closer.

"Car, what's going on?"

Carson didn't answer her as she inched closer to the water's edge. The wind grew stronger, freezing Carson in her tracks. She dropped her flashlight at the sound of a breaking twig.

She fell to her knees to retrieve the flashlight.

"Abby, flash your light."

Abby aimed her light toward the ground. Her eyes locked with a raccoon's and stayed glued until the creature decided to hightail it up a tree. The shining light wavered in her shaking hands.

"Car, I've had enough. Let's go."

Carson finally found her flashlight and stood up. The wind stopped, but she could still feel its icy breath across her skin. *What the hell is that?* she wondered.

"Carson?"

She turned to Abby, took one look at her ashen face, and decided they needed to go home.

"Okay, I'm with you. Just give me one second." She turned her light once more to the spot that the raccoon had occupied. Nothing but dead grass and gravel flickered in the light. A heavy sigh escaped her lips as she probed the light in a circle, hoping something would appear. She looked back to Abby, her arms clasped across her midsection.

Carson's shoulders slumped. It was time to give up. Slowly, she started to pull the flashlight from the area when the light reflected off something shiny.

She rushed toward the tree, pointing her light on the object. A driver's license was partially hidden in the grass. Carson bent down and picked it up, placing it under the light.

Emily's face stared back at her.

"Carson, what is it?"

"It's . . ."

The blaring of a car horn ripped through the silence. "Shit, that's Jamie."

Abby turned to go.

Carson looked back out at the lake. She couldn't leave now. She was close to something. Maybe if she had just a few more minutes. She sighed and turned to Abby.

A sudden gust of wind charged the air, rapping itself around her, begging her to stay.

"Car, come on. Jamie's in trouble."

She didn't move. The cloaklike wind forced her to stay, pulling her toward the lake.

"Carson!"

Carson shook off the cold. Concern marred Abby's features. She ignored the look. "Let's get out of here."

They flashed the beams wildly ahead of themselves so they wouldn't trip as they flailed through the woods to get to Jamie.

They reached the metal barrier and skidded to a halt. Headlights from a park ranger's truck illuminated Jamie's car.

Carson saw Jamie's hands tremble as they gripped the steering wheel. The ranger leaned into the window, talking to a quaking Jamie.

Carson felt her anger rise against the Neanderthal who seemed intent on scaring her friend. With fisted hands, she climbed over the gate and headed to the car. Before she could reach it, the ranger straightened and pointed his flashlight directly into Carson's eyes. She uncurled her fist and raised her hand to block the light.

"Stop right there."

"Sir, could you please not point that thing in my eyes?"

Ignoring her, he asked Jamie, "Are these the friends you were telling me about?"

"Ye-yes."

"Okay, ladies. You"—he pointed toward Abby—"get in the car with your friend here, and you"—he flashed the light back into Carson's face—"you ride with me." He turned the beam away from her and flashed it toward the ranger Jeep an inch away from Jamie's bumper.

Abby jumped into the passenger seat while Carson stayed glued to her spot.

"And where are you taking us?"

"I'm taking you and your friends to the ranger's station. Now get in the truck." He moved away from Jamie's window toward the back end of the car.

Carson felt some of her haughtiness wane. The man had to be at least six feet four. His dark brown bomber jacket made it impossible to tell how much of his bulky upper body was him and how much was jacket. She couldn't really see his face because his ranger hat was pulled down close to his eyes. Intimidation. Jeez, what was it with her sudden run-in with hot, macho meatheads?

"Why should I go with you?" She crossed her arms.

He stopped and flashed the light back in her eyes. "How about trespassing? Public disturbance? Who knows, maybe you and your buddies are doing drugs? Already had one death here, and there isn't going to be another one. Not on my watch. Now get in the car."

"We're not trespassing. This is a public park." She smirked.

"That's closed after dark. Therefore, you are trespassing."

"It was a simple mistake? We didn't know that after-dark rule. So I think you should let us go, and we can forget about the whole thing."

"Simple mistake? Yeah, I can see that. I can see how you missed this big sign." He pointed to the huge wooden barrier to the right of the gate, and it stated the parks hours. "And a five-inch, chain-padlocked gate can be a little misleading. I bet you guys had no idea you were breaking the law. Maybe I should just let you go." He scratched his head. "Or better yet, since you seem to be the ringleader of this little group, why don't I let your accomplices go and just keep you here by yourself, how about that?"

The idea of being stuck all alone in the dark woods with this man crushed her hoity-toity attitude. She lowered her arms and obeyed the order. After a few minutes of riding in the Jeep, Carson vowed never to own or drive a Jeep again. She knew she'd have some bruises from all the jarring her body took as the Jeep climbed up steep, rocky terrain. She'd been too busy holding on to the roll bar that she never once spoke to or looked at rocking ranger. Within minutes, which seemed like an eternity, the ranger pulled his truck alongside a log cabin stilted into the side of the mountain. Motion-detector floodlights bathed the tiny station in bright rays.

He turned off the Jeep and turned toward her. "Do you want—"

"Oh my god. You're like twelve." She stared at his boyish perfect face.

"Excuse me."

"You look like you're twelve years old. And to think I was intimidated by you." She climbed out of the Jeep.

He jumped out of the driver's side and caught her by the arm. "Where do you think you're going?"

"Nowhere?"

He released her. "Okay, good, that's what I thought. And just for the record, I'm twenty-eight years old."

"Okay."

"Go up to the station. I'll wait for your cohorts. It's pretty damn cold out here."

"It's not that cold, I'll stay here, thanks."

Carson stood in silence, watching as Jamie's little beater chugged up the terrain.

The air grew colder and penetrated her sweatshirt. She rubbed her hands up and down her arms. As soon as the ranger looked toward her, she stopped. She couldn't let him get one up on her. If he could handle the cold, so could she, sort of. She cursed her stubborn hide.

The hard planes of his face softened as he smiled. It reached his eyes, which made him look even younger than twelve.

"Go inside, it's cold out here."

Carson refused to move.

"You have got to be the most mule-headed woman I have ever met."

"I don't know what you're talking about, Sir Ranger."

"Go inside." The youthful smile was gone. She turned on her heel and climbed up the short flight of stairs and opened the door. A blast of heat hit her as she entered the cabin. She scanned the medium-size room. A desk sat in the corner, facing a little jail cell. A two-way radio, perched upon a filing cabinet in the other corner, buzzed. A small pot-bellied stove stood in the middle of the room, causing the toasty atmosphere.

Carson walked over to the stove and placed her hands on top of it, trying to get warm. Once the tingling left her fingers, she reached into her pocket and pulled out Emily's license.

Emily's image stared back at her, yet it wasn't the Emily Carson she knew. Her hair was almost white, and her skin was way too dark. The shade of red lipstick was not Emily. Em had only ever worn light pinks and glosses. And there was something about her eyes. There was a sad glint to them. No joy radiated from her face. Carson couldn't remember a time when Emily wasn't happy or full of energy and life.

But this picture lacked the essence that was Emily. Had she left her boyfriend? Did she fear for her life? She looked at the expiration date. The license was less than a year old. That meant that Emily came back to Tennessee twice, and neither time did she call her best friend.

BJ's words echoed in her head, "Carson, people sometimes aren't who we think they are." She glanced back at the picture. *What happened to you? Who did you become?*

The sound of the door opening startled Carson, and she quickly shoved the license back into her pocket.

"Carson." Jamie and Abby hurried toward her.

Her friends both embraced her, and after a quick hug, she pulled away from them. "Here, warm yourselves by the stove."

"I'll be back in about ten minutes." All three turned at the sound of the ranger's voice. "Try not to get yourselves into any more trouble." He started to shut the door.

"You're going to leave us here? You can't do that." Carson accused.

The little-boy smile appeared on his lips once more. "Oh, I can and I will." He shut the door, locking it.

Abby and Jamie looked at Carson, their expressions saying what-now. Carson rushed to the door to pull it open. "Dammit." She smacked her hand against the door. "He locked us in." Scanning the room once more, she saw a small window in the jail cell she hadn't noticed earlier.

"I think we can climb out this window." She turned back to Abby and Jamie. "We'll just jump in the car. He doesn't know who we are."

"Yes, he does."

"What? No, I didn't give him any identification."

"But I did," Jamie spoke. "I was scared, I told him all of our names."

"That's just great."

"It doesn't matter anyway," Abby piped in. "Mr. Boy Ranger took Jamie's keys."

"Great."

"Oh god, what are we going to do?" Jamie started to cry. "I can't go to jail. I have a baby and a husband. Oh no, Tommy. He's going to kill me. What if he leaves me? What will I do?"

"Will you stop your whining? You're pathetic," Abby said.

Jamie spoke between gasps. "No, you're pathetic. This was your stupid idea in the first place. Come on, let's help Carson play detective," she mimicked. "It'll be fun. So are you having fun now? Huh, Abby?"

"Hey, guys, stop." Carson stepped between her friends. "If anyone is to blame, it's me. I'm sorry I dragged you into this. I just . . . I've already lost one friend. I don't want to lose you guys too."

Abby and Jamie looked at each other then at Carson. They both embraced her.

"You're not going to lose us," Jamie said.

"Yeah, in fact we're going to be roommates for a while," this was from Abby.

"Thanks, guys. I promise I'll get us out of this. Once that little boy comes back, I'll make him let us go. He has no right to keep us."

"Where do you think he went?" Jamie asked.

"I don't know." Carson rubbed her temples. "But I don't think he can keep us here. We haven't done anything."

"Yeah, but you didn't do anything yesterday, and Hunter kept you in jail for three hours," Jamie mentioned.

"That's it." Carson snapped her fingers. "Jamie, you're brilliant. I'll just tell him that I'm real tight with the best detective in Nashville. It's perfect. I'll throw Hunter Reeves's name around, and he'll have no choice but to let us go."

"Well, I'm glad to know I'm good for something."

Carson rolled her eyes and let her head flop back then swore before she turned to the door to face Hunter.

Chapter 14

Carson quickly pulled her gaze away from Hunter's. She looked at her friends. Jamie had a stupid smile on her face, and Abby smiled at her then mouthed wow.

Carson gritted her teeth and balled her hands into fists to stifle her urge to scream. "How did you find me?"

"Where did you put it?"

"Put it?" He unfolded his arms.

"The tracking device. Is it in my clothes?" She pulled on her sweatshirt, shaking it while simultaneously pulling on her pants legs. "Did you slip it in my clothes last night before you snuck away?"

"You spent the night with him last night?" Abby and Jamie cooed.

Hunter kept his eyes locked on Carson. "I have no idea what you're talking about."

"Really? Then how did you find me?"

The door banged open, and Boy Ranger joined the group.

"Detective Reeves, you got here pretty quick."

Hunter's eyes bored into Carson. "I wasn't that far away."

Carson refused to hold his glare. She knew more than likely that he had waited at her house.

"Well, you told me to report to you if there was anything odd going on around here. I found these three ladies. I checked the car, but there's nothing there except a few baby bottles and parenting books."

"Thanks, Peter. I'll take it from here." Hunter stepped forward, and Carson stepped back.

"Stay away from me."

"Stay away from you. I ought to wring your skinny little neck." He flexed his fingers.

"Excuse me." Abby tapped Hunter's left shoulder.

His eyes grazed over the top of his shoulder. "Could you give us a minute?"

"Huh, no. You see us being here is all my fault."

"And you are?"

"Hi, I'm Abby." She smiled. "Carson's good friend from New Orleans and now her temporary roommate."

Hunter cocked his left eyebrow and then turned to Carson. "Roommate, huh." He turned back to Abby and Jamie.

"Explain." He raised his hand in silence as both girls tried to speak at the same time. "One at a time."

Abby spoke up, "We were going to go back to Car's place, but she has this ant problem—"

"Abby," Carson warned.

"Ant problem." He smiled.

"Yes, it seems I've been having a problem with pests these days. They just won't seem to leave me alone. So I figured a little poison could get rid of them." Carson crossed her arms, daring Hunter to say something.

"Excuse me, I'm talking here." Abby butted in. "As I was saying, I just got into town, and I begged Carson to show me where you guys found Emily. See, I'm a suspense writer, and I thought it would make a good story."

Carson and Jamie's jaws dropped.

"I love a good mystery. What have you written?" Hunter asked.

"Written? Nothing yet. I'm in the beginning stages, you know. Maybe we could go out to lunch sometime, and you can tell me all about being a cop. I could use you in my book."

"Right."

"How about now? We'll go get some coffee."

"Some other time, I need a private word with your friend here." Hunter turned away from Abby and focused on Carson. He grabbed her arm and propelled her into the cell.

"That was rude," Carson spoke.

"You promised me. You gave me your word you'd let me handle this."

"I don't know—"

"Can it, Carson. What the hell were the three of you doing here?"

"I don't know what you're talking about. Like she said, she's writing a book."

Hunter dropped her arm. "If she's a writer, then I just became the new police commissioner."

"Really, I didn't know you were up for a promotion. Congratulations."

"Dammit, Carson, this isn't a fucking game. Do you know what went through my mind when Peter called me and I ran a check on the license plate? I envisioned fishing your body out of the lake and burying you next to your dead friend."

Carson raised her hand to touch his cheek, but he pulled away. "Hunter, I—"

"You lied to me. For a just a little bit, I believed you were different than most women. But I think you're worse. You stared me right in the eye, didn't even flinch as you lied through your pretty little teeth."

Carson flinched as though she'd been slapped. "I didn't actually lie. I had my fingers crossed. That's different, right?"

"Yeah, I think it's different," Jamie called out.

"Way different," Abby added.

He closed his eyes and shook his head.

"Hunter?"

He looked at Carson. "What?"

"Are you going to stop working on the case?"

"No, Carson, unlike you, my word is my word."

Carson flinched. His words cutting deep. She always prided herself of being a woman of her word. But this was different, wasn't it?

"You have nothing to say?"

Was that a plea Carson detected in his voice? She started to apologize, but instead she answered, "I remembered something that might help."

"What's that?"

"Emily's afraid of the dark."

"And?"

"Well, doesn't that prove there was no way she'd come here in the middle of the night alone?"

"No, it doesn't." He sighed.

"Well, it proves it to me."

"The only thing that's been proven to me is that I can't trust you. So you've just earned yourself a bodyguard."

"That's silly." Carson laughed. "You can't hire someone to watch me."

"Oh, not just someone. Me. Starting tonight. I'll go home, pack a bag, and be at your house in an hour."

"What? You can't stay at my house, Abby is."

"Won't be a problem. I'll take the couch, and Abby can share your bed. It's big enough."

Carson's cheeks grew warm at his innuendo that he'd been in her bed. She didn't dare look at her pals to see the smiles on their face. Unjust as they'd be.

"No, this is ludicrous. You aren't—"

He pulled her close, whispering in her ear, "What's the matter, Carson, afraid you might not be able to keep your hands off me?"

"If anything, it's you who'll have the problem," she hissed through her teeth.

"No, you see there's one thing you don't know about me. I don't sleep with manipulators. They tend to be dangerous." He backed away.

"How dare you—"

"You have one hour to get home, all of you."

"I'm not letting you in my house."

"I doubt that, Carson. You've proven to me all you care about is finding Emily's killer, and you'll do anything"—he made a point to examine her body—"to get it solved."

"You'll be home in one hour." He stormed out the door.

Carson wrung her hands as she paced her small living room. How was she going to live with Hunter in her house? Especially now, he hated her. A chill raced up her spine as she recalled the way Hunter's warm aquamarine eyes darkened like the red-blue flicker of a flame when he looked at her. And it wasn't passion this time, it was loathing. A manipulator? That wasn't her at all; if anything, he's the manipulator. Opening the case just to get her into bed. If anyone had a right to be angry, it was her. The more she thought about it, the angrier she became.

"Carson, will you sit down? You are driving me crazy." Abby had the recliner fully back.

"How can I? That snake's going to be here any minute."

"No, he's going to be here in fifteen minutes. And frankly, I'm glad. I feel a whole lot safer knowing he's sleeping on this couch. I have to be honest, going to the lake really crept me out."

"Okay, Ms. Mystery Writer. What was that all about?"

"I had to think of something. It worked, didn't it?"

"No. He knew you were lying."

"Well, maybe I will become a writer."

"Whatever. You'd make a better Benedict Arnold."

"What's that supposed to mean?"

"You and Jamie are supposed to be my friends. But as soon as you got a look at Hunter, you hung on his every word. You practically drooled all over him."

"For someone who doesn't like the man, she sure sounds jealous?"

"Hardly, the guy's a cretin." Carson curled her upper lip.

"I don't know what your problem is. The man's gorgeous. Did you see the way those Levi's clung to his ass. Whoa. And that incredible specimen wants you. I'll tell you, if I didn't have Gary, I'd be all over that." Abby sat up in the recliner.

"You can have him."

"I have a great idea. How about in the middle of the night I come out here, wake up Hunter, tell him I can't possibly sleep in the same bed with you, and ask him for the couch. Being a gentleman that he is, he'll let me have it; and who knows, maybe he'll crawl into your bed."

Carson knew Abby was way off base, but then again, his promise not to touch her was for her ears only. "I wouldn't sleep with that man if he was the last man on earth."

"Don't worry, it won't be an option."

Abby and Carson screamed at the sound of Hunter's voice.

"Dammit. Have you always had this nasty habit of sneaking up on people and eavesdropping on their conversations?" Carson accused.

Hunter shrugged his shoulders. "Maybe people shouldn't talk about stuff they don't want overheard." He walked past Carson without even a glance and tossed his bag on the couch. Kicking off his shoes, he sat on the couch and planted his feet on top of the coffee table. "What are we watching?"

Abby smiled at him. "*E! Hollywood* ranks the most eligible bachelors. But I haven't seen too much since someone has been distracting me."

"Who ranks these guys?" Hunter asked.

"I think Hollywood does. Who knows? Would you like something to drink?" Abby started to get up.

"Don't get up. I'll get it."

"It's no problem. At least one of us could play the gracious hostess."

Carson wanted to scream, "No, he couldn't have anything to drink"; but the words never materialized. That would make her look like a spoiled child. She wouldn't let Hunter have a chance to call her a brat. She'd just ignore him and her ex-friend, Abby. Once this case was solved and Hunter was out of her life, she might consider being her friend again.

But as she watched Abby bounce back into the living room, she rescinded the offer.

"I don't know what you could drink, so I brought a beer and a diet root beer."

"I'll take the beer. I'm on leave, so it won't hurt to indulge a little bit."

"What do you mean you're on leave?" Carson asked.

His gaze never left Abby's. "I was due a few weeks of vacation. I decided now would be as good a time as any to take it. That way, I can devote all my time to Emily's case." He sipped his beer.

"And how do you plan to do that if you're not at the police station?" Suspicion clouded Carson's mind.

"I don't need to be in the police station."

"Of course you don't because you have no intention of helping me."

"Not this again."

"Yes, this again." Carson pointed her finger at him. "The more I think about it, I realized I didn't do anything wrong. This is all your fault."

"What?" He placed his beer down. "You lied to me."

"Yes, but only after you lied first. Therefore, I'm right and you're wrong."

"No, I never lied to you, so you're wrong."

"You only pretended to open Em's case so you could get me in bed, and then when I caught you, you had no choice but to open it."

"I think this is my cue to leave." Abby headed to the bedroom.

Carson grabbed her arm. "Oh no, you don't. You sit right here. I want you to see firsthand just what a hero this guy isn't."

"Speaking of that whole 'I'm opening the case to get you in bed'"—he stood up—"who told you that bullshit?"

"It's not bullshit. B . . . I thought of it on my own."

"BJ, I should have known."

"I never said . . ."

"You're gullible, you know that. You sit there and listen to this petty PI about my intentions. When in fact, he's the one who wants to get you in bed, and he's trying to make me out to be the bad guy. And it worked."

"That's absurd. BJ doesn't want to sleep with me. I've known him forever. He's a good friend. A trustworthy friend."

"Um, we'll see." He picked up his beer.

"What's that supposed to me?"

"Just don't come running to me when your trustworthy, honorable BJ makes a pass. Okay?"

"Don't worry because it won't ever happen." Carson turned to Abby. "What do you think of your so-called hero now? You know BJ, and you know he's way off base."

Abby pulled her arm free and headed to the recliner. "All I know is that you both should just sleep together and move on."

"I'm going to bed," Carson said, but she didn't move from her spot. "I said I'm going to bed."

"We heard you. Good night," Abby said.

"Aren't you coming, Abby?"

"No. It's too early for bed. Besides that, I'm not tired."

"Fine. But don't think you can crawl into bed late and wake me up. I have to work tomorrow." She closed herself in her room.

Carson pulled the blanket up to her neck and rolled to the left, pulling her legs up into her chest. A sigh escaped her lips as she switched positions to the right side. She curled the pillow in half to give her head better elevation. The clock's red numbers glowed at her. It was only nine o'clock. There was no way she could sleep this early. Giving up, she rolled on her back, put her hands behind her head, and stared up at the ceiling. The sound of the TV came through the wall. She tried to listen to their conversation, but all she heard were mumbled whispers then an occasional laugh from Hunter.

She couldn't recall if she'd ever heard him laugh before. As grating as it was, the sound also sent a shivering sensation down her spine.

"Ugh." She grabbed the pillow and covered her face. Maybe if she were lucky, she would accidentally smother herself, and then this nightmare would be over.

Chapter 15

Carson covered her mouth to stifle her tenth yawn in a matter of minutes. Exhaustion radiated through her body. Between Saturday night and last night, she'd barely gotten ten hours of sleep. The cause sat at the corner of the bar, watching her every move.

Hunter drove her to work then parked his butt at the end of the bar, and he'd been there ever since. The man wasn't kidding when he said she had herself a bodyguard. Guard dog was more like it. He eyed everyone that came to the bar, occasionally writing a note here and there.

Carson had hoped that she and Hunter could get down to Emily's case, but the lunch shift had been extra busy today, leaving her no time to talk to Hunter. Yet now that she had the time, she couldn't quite look him in the eye after this morning.

It had been about two in the morning, and she'd been on the verge of falling asleep before Abby chose that precise moment to stumble into bed. They battled for the covers for a few minutes; then Abby was out for the count. To make matters worse, she tossed all around the bed and snored. Carson remembered the scheme Abby had concocted earlier about getting her and Hunter in the same bed. Suddenly, she wondered if this was her sleep behavior, or had she decided to put her plan into action? She elbowed Abby in the back until she was on her side. The snoring stopped, but sleep evaded Carson.

When she rolled out of bed at dawn, she knew she was in for a hell of a day. Her eyes half-closed, she willed her feet to take her to the kitchen. The smell of vanilla-hazelnut coffee tickled her nose. That's funny, she didn't remember setting the coffeepot.

"Well, good morning."

Carson's eyes popped open. Hunter stood in the kitchen doorway, showered and perfect, with a cup of coffee in his hands. Oh god, she'd forgotten he lived here now.

"I like your sleep attire."

She looked down at her nightshirt that had a giant hole in the middle and barely touched the top of her thighs. She squatted down, trying the pull the shirt over her knees as she waddled backward into her room. Hunter's leering grin never veering away.

"Car, where is this going? Yoo-hoo, Carson."

Carson shook this morning's event from her mind. "What?"

"Who's eating this grilled chicken with orzo rice?"

"I—"

"That's mine." Hunter called from his end of the bar.

Carson's mouth hung open while she watched Derek take the food and place it in front of him. Etiquette and common sense flew out the window. She charged down the bar, tripping over the hose that snaked out from under the sink. She righted herself before she fell completely on her face.

"How did you get that?"

"That nice little waitress ordered it for me."

Carson looked over at the waitress Shari, who watched Hunter with her tongue hanging out of her mouth and a lovesick expression on her face.

"You'll seduce anything." She knew it was lack of asleep that made her irrational.

"Darling, I'm just a growing man who needs some nourishment. Besides, I am a paying customer." He shoveled a piece of chicken in his mouth.

"You are not a guest. You are a . . . a . . . a . . ."

"Customer."

"No, you're not."

"No. You have a new customer at your bar." With the knife in his hand, he pointed over her shoulder.

"What?" She turned to the top of the bar. Henry had taken a seat. Good, she needed the distraction. On her way to greet him, she stopped at the beer cooler, pulled out a Miller Lite, and placed it in front of him.

"Henry, it's so good to see you. Where have you been all week?"

A look of dismay crossed her face as she watched him take a pack of cigarettes out his pocket and placed them on top of the bar. "You're smoking again?" She placed an ashtray in front of him.

"Yeah."

"But you've done so good."

"Well, that was before the missus took me down to Florida for a week. Looking at retirement communities. Says she's tired of the weather changes, wants hot weather all year around. I tell you one thing, I ain't going nowhere. She can go without me. Suit me just fine."

"Oh, you don't mean that. You'd be lost without her." She placed a fresh napkin under his beer.

"Nah, because if I was twenty years younger"—he looked over her shoulder before he continued—"I wouldn't stand a chance."

What? That's not how the saying goes. Carson wondered if he was okay. Maybe he'd spent too much time in the Florida sun.

"That your boyfriend down there?"

Carson rolled her eyes. "That guy. No way."

"He sure looks at you like you're his girlfriend. The guy hasn't taken his eyes off you since you came down here. Well, I'd better get going."

"But you didn't finish your beer."

"Got to get home."

"Don't be a stranger," she yelled out to him and then marched back down to the end of the bar.

"You scared my customer away. Why don't you just leave and come back in an hour when my shift is done." She needed to get back her sanity. She didn't want to think about the fact that she could get used to having him watch her all day. Damn her overexhausted brain.

"You know." He placed his silverware on his plate. "For someone so hell-bent on finding a killer, you're doing a lousy job."

"What are you talking about?"

"You've been pretty busy, I'll grant you that much; but now is the perfect time to go over our notes, and you want me to leave. I'm here to help you with Emily's case. That is what you wanted, right?"

Carson knew he was right. She was being a silly little fool. This wasn't about her. It was about Emily, but she couldn't think straight around this man. She wanted her wits about her when they talked about Emily, and they would talk about Emily as soon as she escaped him and checked one more thing out.

Her shift was coming to an end. She needed to find a way out of there and leave Hunter behind. But that'd be impossible since he insisted on driving in with her. She had to think of something. Grabbing her money and paperwork, she stepped out from behind the bar. A glance at Hunter saw him raising from his chair.

"Take it easy, Tonto. I have to go in the back and do my money. I'll only be about twenty to thirty minutes at the most."

The perfect plan formed in her mind on her way back to the office. Jamie was still there. This could work.

"Jamie, I need a huge favor."

"No way, no more favors." She didn't look away from her computer.

"Jamie, please I'm desperate."

"Aren't you always?"

"I need to borrow your car."

"What?" Jamie looked at her this time. Carson noted the dark smudges under her eyes and felt terrible. She should have never dragged her to the lake last night. Nor should she put her in this position, but she'd make it up to her later.

"I can't lend you my car, I'm leaving in about thirty minutes."

"That's fine. Hunter's out there. As soon as you're done, he can take you home."

"Oh no. I don't want any part of that."

"Please, I'm desperate. He's been in my hair since last night. All I need is a little time alone. I know you know what it's like not to have any time to yourself. Please, please, please."

"After last night, I don't want that man on my bad side."

"It won't be your bad side, it'll be mine."

"Carson, why don't you just have him drive you home and ask him to leave because you need some time alone."

"Well, I'm not actually going home."

"Carson!" She tossed her pen on the desk.

"Jamie, please. I won't ask you for any more favors."

"This is about Emily, isn't it? You got what you want. You have Hunter helping you now, so why aren't you letting him help you?"

"I do want his help. It's just that—"

"I don't like this new person you are."

"What's that mean?"

"It means the Carson I know and love has never been purposely mean to anyone."

"I'm not being mean. It's just that I found something last night."

"What? And you didn't tell me. What was it?"

"No." She shook her head. "The less you know, the safer you are from Hunter's third degree."

"You need to share this with Hunter before it blows up in your face."

"Don't you see I can't? I mean I had opportunity to tell him last night, but everything got so complicated, and it never came up. If I go to him now, he'll think I was hiding it from him and accuse me of being a manipulator again. I just need to check this out, and it will be the last time I keep Hunter in the dark."

"What if it's dangerous?"

Carson knew that Jessie was bending. "Believe me when I say I'm in no danger. Besides, it'll probably pan out to be nothing."

"I don't know, Carson. I don't know if I can trust you when you say you're not in danger. Your track recorded hasn't been so great recently."

Carson ignored the barb. "So you'll do it?"

She swiveled in her chair. "Something tells me I'm doing the wrong thing." She pulled her purse from under the desk, searched through it, then handed Carson the keys. "Here. But this is the last time."

Carson snatched the keys. "Thanks, you're the best." She leapt from her chair and headed out the door.

"Hey."

Carson popped her head back in.

"What about your bank?"

"Do you mind?"

"Get out of here. But you owe me big time and not just for today."

It took Carson twenty minutes to reach the Department of Motor Vehicles. Jessie was probably telling Hunter right now that she needed a ride. She hoped Jessie was okay. If Hunter scared Jessie even just a little bit, he'd have to answer to her.

She entered the one-time trailer home that now housed the DMV. No matter what time of the day, the place was always packed. Six chairs lined the left and the right walls while a set of ten chairs, back-to-back, filled the middle. Two teenage boys, along with their father, sat along the left side. Six immigrant construction workers with one man as a translator inhabited the middle row of chairs. An older married couple occupied the right side along with an overdue pregnant mother.

She walked over to the counter. A gray-haired, tiny spec of a woman sat on the other side with the telephone pressed to her ear.

"Hold on," the woman spoke into the receiver. "Go down there, get your number, and fill out the paperwork from that table over there."

"Well, I actually need to talk to someone."

"Is it about a license?"

"Sorta."

The older woman rolled her eyes. "Sweetie, there's no sorta. We're the DMV. We deal with picture IDs."

"I know that. It's—"

"Then do as I said, and you'll come up when your number's called."

"But you see this is important."

"Honey, it's always important. 'But it's my son's first license, can't you push us through?' 'I'm really running late to work, could you get me in first?' 'I swear I didn't know it expired last month.' So please, it's been a long day; so if you don't mind doing me a favor, be a good girl and wait for your turn." She shooed her away before turning back to her phone conversation.

Feeling as though she'd just been scolded by her grandmother, Carson walked toward the little white machine, pressed a button, and grabbed the little white piece of paper that quoted her as number 95 A. She looked up at the electronic board. It read 82 A. Great.

Deeply engrossed in the latest issue of *Entertainment* magazine and an article about her favorite actress, Carson's number was called three times before she heard it. She looked around the deserted office. Everyone was gone.

She walked up to the counter.

"Just sign the line and sit over in that chair."

"I'm not here to get a license. It's police business."

"Police business? You don't look like any of the cops I know. Does she look like a cop to you, May?"

Carson glanced up at the gray-haired woman who scolded her earlier. May raised an eyebrow. "She doesn't look like a cop."

Carson cleared her throat. "I'm not a cop, I'm a private detective." She fumbled in her purse and took out Em's license. "I need to know if either one of you ladies remembers this girl."

"Honey, do you know how many IDs we snap in a day? Well over a hundred. How are we going to remember one girl?"

She held out the license. "This was taken about two months ago. Could you please just look."

The lady sitting behind the desk took the ID. "Doesn't look familiar to me. How bout you, May?"

May sighed before taking the picture. "I don't know, maybe."

"What do you mean maybe?" Carson asked. "Do you remember her or not?"

"I said maybe. What's it matter?" She handed the license back to Carson.

"It matters a lot. She was murdered a couple of weeks ago."

"Oh my." May's hand went to her neck.

"Please tell me you remember her." Carson watched May examine the picture with excited anticipation. Then like the sails of a ship dying in the wind, so did her hopes as the woman shook her head.

"May, maybe I should look at it again." The other woman held out her hand.

"Uh . . . sure, here you . . . oops." May dropped the license. Both ladies bent down to pick it up. Carson tried to look over the counter when she heard them whispering. She hadn't heard a word as both women pooped back up.

"Like May said, we do over a hundred a day." The lady handed the license back.

"Here's my card." She placed it on top of the counter. "If anything comes to mind at all, please contact me at anytime." She reached the door and looked back one last time. The sight of the two ladies arguing made her wish she'd have trusted Hunter.

Chapter 16

"Stupid, stupid, stupid." Carson beat the steering wheel. She screwed up. Those ladies knew something. But because of her inexperience and vain attempt to prove she didn't need Hunter, she probably scared them away. Now what was she going to do? She stared out the windshield at Jamie's house. She knew she needed to go in and face the music. And just as she thought it, Hunter barreled down the steps.

He flung open the car door, killed the ignition, then hauled her out of the car.

He shook her. "Where the hell have you been?"

"I—"

He released her. "I went to the lake, to your apartment, to BJ's. No one knew where you were!" He paced in front of her while raking a hand through his hair. He stopped his pacing. "You were working on Emily's case."

Carson averted eye contact as she nodded her head.

"You little idiot. You insist on putting yourself in danger."

"I wasn't in any danger. I was at the Motor Vehicles."

"What?"

"I had a lead that led me to the DMV. I thought I could—"

"Show me what you have."

"It's—"

He grabbed her. "No more games, Carson, give it to me."

She shuddered at the anger that radiated from his blue gaze. "If you'd release me, I'd be happy to."

He let go, and she fished the license from her purse.

"I found this at the lake last night."

He plucked the ID from her fingers and stared at it. His lips came together, forming a straight white line. "Where exactly did you find this?"

"The entrance where they found Em's body. You and your men must have missed it."

"No, Carson, we didn't miss it because it wasn't there. We searched that area three times."

"Well, apparently you missed a spot because I found it."

"Do you know what this means?"

"You should have searched four times." She attempted to smile.

"No, it means the killer knows you're looking into this case. It means you've shaken him up."

"No, it only means I found something your guys missed." She rubbed her arms.

"You found it because the killer must have gone back and put there. And any hopes of finding fingerprints are gone because you've handled, and now I've handled it, and God only knows who else you let touch it." The license appeared to be paper as his blunt fingers snapped it in half.

"I didn't even think—"

"Of course, you didn't. Because I'm the cop, and you're the bartender. It's not in your nature to think."

She closed her eyes, willing the tears to stay hidden. She didn't want him to know how bad his words had hurt her. And she didn't want to analyze her reaction either.

"Why didn't you show me this last night? I may have been able to salvage something from it."

"I was trying to help."

"No, you were trying to outwit me. God only knows why. I'm not the enemy, Carson, although you like to think that I am."

She thought she detected sadness in his voice but dismissed the idea. And she didn't deny that he was wrong. She had distinguished him as the enemy because if she hadn't, she'd might do something stupid like fall in love. *Oh crap, where had that come from?*

"I'm sorry, you're right. I screwed up. I think those DMV ladies recognized Emily. And maybe if I would have confided in you, we'd be closer to finding Em's killer."

"What happened?"

Carson reiterated her DMV fiasco.

"Carson, what else are you keeping from me?"

Now was the time to be honest and tell him about the little boy from the lake. "Well . . ."

"Hold that thought." Hunter grabbed the beeper from his belt and read the number. He attached it back to his belt and looked up at her. "Go give Jamie her keys. Then I'm taking you home."

The short five-minute drive to her house resembled the five-hour trips she'd take with her family during the summers.

Neither spoke as they trudged the stairs to her apartment. The sound of the TV could be heard in the hall. That was Abby, always had to have things big and loud. The smile she felt refused to surface for fear that Hunter would take it the wrong way. To fight with Hunter would be like taking a rubber band and snapping it against her wrist, a self-inflicted pain.

Abby, asleep on the couch when they entered, sprung up when the door slammed closed.

"What?" She used the palm of her hand to wipe the drool from her mouth.

"Hey, Abby, it's just us." Carson headed toward Abby while Hunter went to the kitchen and used the phone.

"It's about time you two got home. I'm hungry, but I was waiting for you guys before I ate."

Carson wanted to tell her friend she wasn't hungry, but the sudden rumble of her tummy was loud enough to drown out the sound of the TV. So much for hiding in her room, away from him, the rest of the night.

"Yeah, I'm hungry."

Hunter came out of the kitchen. "Something's come up, I have to go."

Carson looked at him. "Where are you going? Is it about Em?"

Hunter ignored her as he strode to the key holder next to the phone, snatching her and Abby's keys from their rings then dropping them into his pocket.

"What are you doing?"

"What's it look like. I'm taking your keys and Abby's."

"Why?"

"Because I don't know how long I'm going to be gone. And I don't trust you to stay put and out of trouble."

"Why don't I come with you?" Carson asked.

"I think you've done enough damage tonight, haven't you?" The soft click of the closing door sounded more like a building coming down during a demolition.

"Should we get pizza then?" Abby grabbed the phone.

"Sure, whatever." Carson stared at the door. What had she done? Would he shut her out now? Did he have a lead on Em's killer? And how bad had she really screwed up? Was all hope of finding Em's killer lost?

"Carson!"

"What?"

"Is pepperoni all right with you?"

"Pepperoni. Order whatever you want, I'm not hungry. I need some fresh air." Carson headed to the door.

"Carson, where are you going? He took our keys. If he wants us to stay put, I'm not gonna cross him."

Carson's hand stilled on the doorknob. "I'm not crossing anyone. I'm just going for a walk. I won't feel like a prisoner in my own home."

"He's not making you a prisoner. He cares about you."

"No, he's being a cop." Carson opened the door.

"At least he's not a sniveling, conniving cop like some that you know."

"Don't even go there, Abby. This is about Hunter trying to control my life."

"No, it's about you not letting go of the past. I really think you can have something with this guy."

"Abby, let it go. And would you for once take my side in something."

"This isn't about sides. I love you, and I want to see some good and happiness come your way."

"The only happiness I'll have is when Hunter is out of my life for good. And that won't happen until Emily's killer is found." She left.

Chapter 17

Some of Carson's anger ebbed as she stood underneath the streetlight. She blew on her hands, wishing she'd grabbed a jacket with pockets instead of a flimsy sweater. It was only early November. Winters were never too bad in Tennessee, except for that one winter of '94. The ice storms that year were awful; some towns were without power for a month. For the most parts, the winter days were quite beautiful; but the nights sometimes got too cold, but not as cold as this night. A gust of wind attacked her. She turned her head away so her hair wouldn't slam into her face.

"Figures. It wouldn't be this cold if I had a car," she yelled to the streetlight. Jumping up and down to keep the blood flowing through her veins, she contemplated going back to the gas station to wait. No sooner had the thought entered her mind than her ride pulled up.

She pulled open the door and jumped in. "Wow, it's cold out there. What took you so long, BJ?"

A smile lit his handsome face. "It hasn't been that long, and I do live fifteen minutes from here."

"You were home. I used your cell phone because I assumed you be out on a case or something."

"Mondays are usually pretty quiet, so it's one of the only nights I can relax at home."

She pressed her hands against the heat vent. "I'm sorry. Why didn't you tell me? I wouldn't have made you come all the way out here."

"That's what friends are for. Besides, you made me nervous. You sounded so upset on the phone. What is going on, and where's your car?"

BJ put his car in gear while Carson filled him in on the latest events in Em's case.

A chill greeted them when they entered BJ's office. BJ flipped on the lights. "Why don't you make some coffee, and I'll check on the heat." He headed down the hall.

Carson walked over to the kitchen area, checked under the cabinet, found the coffee and the filters, and started brewing the coffee. She heard the roaring sound of the heater before she felt the full blast from the vent above her head. While she waited for the coffee to finish, she sleuthed through the outer office. She shuffled through the out-of-date *Time and Sports Illustrated* magazines then discarded them. Hands behind her back, she scanned the plaques on the wall. A beautiful bouquet of flowers sat atop the reception desk. Curiosity got the better of her, and she read the card.

"BJ, thank you for all your help." The signature was bright red lips.

"I must have turned off the heat when I left earlier," BJ yelled from the corridor.

At the sound of his voice, she jumped, crushing the note to her chest. She put the card on the table, trying to smooth out the wrinkles. Knowing it was futile, she placed the card back on the flowers, hoping he wouldn't notice. She then went back to the makeshift kitchen and poured them each a cup of coffee.

"Here you go, black like you like." She handed him a cup.

"Thanks." His gaze focused on her face as he took a sip.

Her right hand went to her hair, and she brushed her fingers from the top of her hairline through and down to the bottom, curling the ends up.

"Why are you nervous?"

"I'm not nervous."

"Yes, you are. You always do that thing with your hair when you're nervous."

"What thing?" Once again she repeated the action.

He smiled. "Let's go into my office, and you can tell me more about the ladies from the DMV."

His private office was small but comforting. She walked around, inspecting it. Two giant file cabinets took up the left corner near the window. A rust-colored leather couch took up the adjacent wall. Next to the couch was a workstation with a computer. She opened a door, expecting a closet but found a bathroom complete with a shower. She looked back at him.

He shrugged. "Sometimes, I don't make it home."

She closed the door and looked over at his desk. Besides a small reading lamp on the corner, the rest of the desk was littered with papers and folders. Three of its legs matched while the back right was two shades lighter.

She inched her way to the desk. "Oh my gosh, that's the same desk you had in college."

"I made my first college A-English paper from that desk and signed my first client there as well. She's my good luck charm."

Carson sat in the leather swivel chair behind the desk. "How do you find anything in this mess?" She started going through the papers on his desk.

"I have my methods. Stop snooping."

"I'm not snoop—" Her hands stilled on the folder she'd just touched. "What is this?"

"Car, it's no—"

Too late, she opened it up. There were crime scene photos and autopsy pictures along with police reports. "Why do you have a file on Emily, and why haven't you told me?" She leafed through the papers with dozens of names and numbers of people she didn't know.

He sighed. "I didn't tell you because there's nothing to tell. I don't have any new information. I planned to tell you as soon as I had something to tell. I didn't want to get your hopes up."

"This doesn't make sense." She pulled a sheet of paper out. "This is a timeline, but it ends with Em going to Hawaii. Then you have a blank and then her death."

"I know."

"What does that mean?"

"It means that I can't find any information on her between those two periods."

"That's impossible. She was in California."

"Are you sure?"

Carson stared up at him.

"Did she ever write you? How often did you guys talk?"

She closed her eyes, trying to think. "Yes, I got a couple of postcards, a few phone calls. But now that I think about it, she always called me collect. She kept telling me she hadn't gotten around to getting a phone."

"There's something else, too, come here."

BJ was at the computer. She got up and joined him.

"I've been doing a lot of Internet searching. This is a surfer Web site. When I click on new surfers, there is no sign of Emily's name anywhere."

"That's not possible." She bent down, peering over his shoulder.

"Most newcomers were guys and only two girls. Susie Barstow and Cherry Brandie."

"Cherry," she whispered.

BJ glanced up at her. "Yeah, Cherry. Carson, what is it?"

"Can you pull up that name?"

He highlighted her name then hit Enter. There weren't any pictures, just a miniscule bio.

Watch out for this newcomer. She's got some great moves, and she's going to give some established surfers a run for their money. This twenty-something beauty splits her time between California and Hawaii. Daughter of a military father who kept them on the move says she never had roots growing up, doesn't plan to plant any now.

Carson hung her head then turned away from him.

BJ stood up. "Car, what's the matter?"

She straightened. "That's Emily."

"What? Em's dad wasn't in the military. She lived here most of her life."

"I know but—" She took a deep breath. "Em and I had this thing we did whenever we went out to the clubs. Whenever certain guys would try to hit on us, we'd tell him our names were Cherry and Brandie and that we were army brats."

He laughed, and she cut him a look. "Sorry. Guys actually fell for those names."

"I don't know, nor do I care."

"Why was she using that name and not her own?" BJ asked.

"So her parents wouldn't find her, I guess."

"Why was she hiding from her parents?"

"They wanted to put her in rehab. That's why she ran off to Hawaii in the first place."

"Why didn't you tell me this?"

"Because I wanted you to help me. Plus, it was Hunter who told me, and I thought he was just saying that to get me off the case. I didn't believe him at the time but now."

"We don't know for sure if that's her."

Carson tilted her head to the side, squinted her eyes in disbelief. "I'd stake my life on it. I just—"

"You just what?"

"I have no idea who Emily was. Nothing makes sense. I don't know which way is up. What the hell is going on?"

BJ put his arms around her, and she welcomed him. It felt good to have someone hold her and let her feel this pain.

His arms tightened their grip. "Car, there's something I need to tell you."

She didn't hear him. Her thoughts focused on the strength of his arms. Had he always been this built? No, she would have remembered. A funny feeling invaded her tummy. BJ had grown up into a sexy man.

"I'm not going to tell you I told you so," Hunter said.

Carson jumped out of BJ's arms and looked into Hunter's accusing grin, remembering his accusation that BJ wanted to bed her.

Chapter 18

Carson felt the heat creep into her face. Guilt assailed her. Then hate for Hunter at making her feel such shame. BJ was one of her dearest friends, a rock she'd leaned on more times than she could count. How dare he cheapen their relationship with his haughty tone and condemning stare. Then she directed her anger to herself for feeling embarrassed.

"Reeves," BJ broke the silence, "you're not interrupting anything."

"Could have fooled me," Hunter accused.

"What can I do for you?"

"I was looking for Carson."

"Well, you found her. Now that you know where she is, you know she's safe. I'll bring her home later."

Hunter didn't move.

"Is there something else I can do for you?"

"Yeah, there are a couple of things you can do. First thing is to stop filling her head with grand ideas of being a PI so she doesn't get herself killed. And second, back off this case, and let me do my job."

"Sorry, can't do that. The lady's hired me as a private investigator, and I plan on helping her."

"Help her what, get killed? You can't protect her the way I can."

"Bravo, Hunter." BJ clapped his hands as the two inched closer to one another. "Aren't you the big strong hero?"

"No, I'm a cop, not a two-bit PI that makes money off other people's dirty laundry."

"The way I see it, the only person she needs protection from is you."

Carson watched the two of them prowling toward one another. A sudden feeling of dread swept over her. Hunter's eyes turned a navy blue. He approached BJ as a panther would an unknowing lamb.

But what frightened her even more was BJ. He was a stranger. In the ten years she'd known him, he never once got angry, let alone ready to hit someone. Always the diplomat, he smoothed ruffled feathers before throwing a punch. His face was beet red, and his hands were fists at his side. His contoured features were a hideous mask of rage.

At first she feared Hunter would make mince meat out of BJ, but now she worried for Hunter's safety. This was all her fault. Once again, she was messing it up. She rushed over and planted herself between the two of them.

She stretched out her arms placing a hand on each one's chest. "Stop it."

"Carson, I suggest you get out of the way," Hunter warned.

"For once, I agree with the man." BJ's body pressed against Carson's hand.

"You're both acting like juveniles. Stop it right now."

"Carson, move." The tone of BJ's voice startled her. His eyes were glazed over with an emotion she couldn't describe. A sudden fear of him caught her off guard.

With a strength she didn't know she possessed, she shoved BJ away from her. His mask of hatred slipped away, and the BJ she knew returned.

He looked down at his clenched fists then back at Carson. "I'm—"

She cut him off, knowing he was about to apologize. She'd never forgive herself if she made him humble himself before Hunter.

"You"—she jabbed her finger into Hunter's chest—"wait for me outside. I'll be out in five minutes."

He didn't budge.

She pointed to the door. "Go, now!"

He left.

She waited until she heard the door close then turned back to BJ. "Are you okay?"

"Car, I'm sorry. I don't, I can't. There's no excuse for my behavior."

Relief flooded her. BJ was back. "What was that all about? I've never seen you so angry. What's the real deal between you and Hunter?"

"There's no . . . it's just I . . . god, I'm sorry."

"BJ, it's okay, don't worry about it."

"No." He shook his head. "I lost control and frightened you. That's unacceptable. It's just that—"

A moment passed. "It's just what?"

"I was mad at myself because what Hunter said was right. I'm putting you in danger, and I should know better."

An alarm bell went off in her head. "What are you saying?"

He sighed. "I'm saying that you should drop this idea of finding Em's killer and let me handle, and if not me, then Hunter. He is the best damn cop I know."

She couldn't believe what she was hearing. Who did these men think they were to dictate how she lived her life? She could expect this type of behavior from Hunter. But now here, her good friend was looking at her, trying to throw his macho beliefs around.

"If you think for one minute, I'm going to let you and your friend Hunter control—"

He raised a hand to interrupt her. "We aren't friends. Far from it, believe me.

"Don't try to change the subject. I'm going to be a key part of this case whether you and your not-so-called friend like or not. Good night." She turned on her heel and left.

The cold air that greeted her when she left the office did little to cool off her anger. Carson couldn't believe she'd have to fight two macho meatheads instead of one. A sudden urgency to find Em's killer and get on with her life flooded her. She didn't know how much more her nerves could take.

She stopped in her tracks at the sight of her car sitting at the curb. Although it was dark, she felt his gaze searing into her. A new anger filled her. The man thought he could just bully his way into her life. It was bad enough he made himself a permanent fixture at her home, but driving her car—that was the last straw.

She ripped open the passenger door and got in her car. "How dare you drive my car? What gives you the right? In fact, get out of my car."

"You are in no position to be giving orders. I can't even take your keys and feel safe enough to trust you. If Abby hadn't called me, God only knows what you two would have done." He put the car in drive.

She refused to let him make her feel guilty again. "Oh no, you don't." She grabbed the gear and pushed it back to park. "It's my car, I drive it."

"Carson, I am warning you."

"Warning me. Hah. No, I'm warning you, you guilt-making macho meathead."

She left her sitting position and got on her knees. Stretching over onto his seat, she reached for the keys. Hunter grabbed her wrist and flipped her so that she was pinned between him and the steering wheel. To struggle was futile since she had nowhere to go. Still in a vain attempt, she tried to yank her wrist free. He tightened his hold and drew her closer. Her face was inches from his.

"You are a piece of work. Why are you fighting me? I just want to keep you safe."

She swallowed hard, knowing what was about to happen. His lips were hard and demanding as they crashed against hers. Then in an instant, they softened; his tongue probing against her mouth, asking for entrance. A whimper sounded from her. She wriggled her hand free of his grasp then ran it through his hair, pushing his head closer, wanting to deepen the kiss.

Carson knew she needed to pull away and stop this from going further. But the heat of his muscled chest melted into her body. Just a few more kisses and she promised she'd get out of this situation. Then his hand cupped her breast, and every thought abandoned her. Nothing had ever felt so good or right to her in her life.

"Carson."

Another whimper escaped her as his warm beautiful lips left hers. But a moan replaced it as his mouth trailed kisses up her stomach and landed on her left breast. Ecstasy filled her. At that moment, she'd give this man whatever he wanted. She leaned back to give him better access. Her body leaned against the horn, shattering the moment.

Sanity returned. She pulled her shirt down and jumped off his lap back into the passenger seat. She refused to look at him.

"I thought you said you wouldn't try anything." She crossed her arms over her chest, refusing to look away from the window.

"If my touching you bothers you so much, I suggest you stop throwing yourself at me."

Her head whirled around. "Throwing myself at you? You attacked me."

"Sugar, I've never had to attack a woman in my life." His gaze lingered on her lips then rested on her breasts.

The slow, lazy drawl of the word *sugar* coming from his mouth cheapened the whole experience. And the thought that he lumped her in the easy category sickened her. Carson wanted to kick herself. She should be glad he did that. It only proved how right she was about him. He was a womanizer, and she would not fall prey to the man.

Chapter 19

Her body still ached in all the places Hunter had touched her. Her fingertips skimmed her lips. No other man ever kissed her that way. He was a magician with his kisses. And she sensed he liked kissing. A lot of men, not that she'd been with a lot, but most of the men she'd dated, liked to bypass the romantic stuff and get right to business. And she was a pure romantic at heart. What was she going to do?

Dumb, dumb, dumb. She needed to stop these crazy thoughts. The man thrived off control. And she, Carson, was a challenge; something he couldn't control. If he ever did bend her to his will, he'd discard like he'd done thirty minutes ago. She shuttered. It had been a long time since a man had made her feel so cheap.

"Yoo-hoo, Carson."

"What?"

"I said are you going to get out of the car?"

They were home. Hunter looked at her with a knowing smile. She pulled her fingers from her lips.

Carson yanked open her door and got out of the car. She wanted to race into the apartment but wouldn't give him the satisfaction. He grabbed her arm and turned her around. Damn, she should have made a break for it.

"You're a very excitable woman, Carson." His knuckles skimmed her cheeks.

For the love of God, she couldn't move her feet. He inched closer, moving in for the kill. *Think, Carson, think.*

"Is it just me, Carson, or are you this way with all men? Do BJ's kisses make you quiver also?"

She sputtered as though she'd been doused in ice-cubed water in February.

"They make me quiver more. In fact, when you kissed me, I closed my eyes and pretended you were BJ."

He laughed as he released her. "Ah, Carson."

"What are you laughing at? It's true."

"Just an hour ago, you defended his honor. Correct me if I'm wrong. But didn't you say you two were just friends, and he'd never do that?"

"I lied." She wanted to wipe that smirk from his face. Their bodies almost touched. She stood on her tiptoes.

"Come on, Hunter. You saw us when you walked into his office. Who knows what would have happened if you hadn't walked in on us." With a smile, she got off her toes and sashayed away from him in satisfaction, knowing that his sly smile was replaced with a look of doubt.

Abby greeted them at the door and bear-hugged Carson.

"Hey, Abby." Carson tried to pull away.

"Oh good, he found you. I was so worried."

"I'm fine, you can let me go."

"Right." Abby pulled her closer and whispered. "We need to talk."

Carson stepped back and looked into her friend's eyes. What was the matter with her? Then she looked at Hunter. He stood, arms crossed, staring them both down.

"Abby, come help me in my room." She tried to pull her away from the door. Hunter grabbed each one by the arm.

"What's going on?"

"Nothing," Abby replied.

"I'm not an idiot. What are you up to?"

"All right." Abby bit her lower lip. "I . . . I think." Then she started crying. Hunter let them go.

"My god, Abby, what is it?" Carson placed her hands on Abby's arms to steady her.

"It's—" Abby cried harder.

"Are you happy now, you big bully? You made her cry." Carson pursed her lips and crinkled her eyes in disgust at Hunter.

"Abby." Hunter cleared his throat.

"It's not him." She wiped her hand across her nose. "I think . . . I think Gary's cheating on me."

"He what?" Carson roared.

"Um, Carson, I think you should take this one. Take her to your room."

"Come on." Carson led Abby to the room. She closed the door and began to pace.

"That slimeball, when I get my hands on him, I'm going to hurt him. Do you know—"

"Carson, give it a rest." Abby stood there, dry-eyed and smiling. "God, that was good, wasn't it? I should be an actress."

"You mean Gary isn't cheating on you?"

"Not if he wants to live to see his next birthday. Besides, the guy's crazy about me."

Carson sat on the bed. "I don't understand."

"I had to think of something. Hunter could see right through me."

"What's going on?"

"Well, after you left, I called Hunter. I had no idea where you ran off to, and I was worried. That part was true. You know you just took off with no car."

"Abby! Get to the point."

"All right already. Jeez. Well, after I called Hunter, this woman called. Let me tell you, she was a weird bird. Whispering and—"

"Abby!" Carson got off the bed.

"It turns out to be some lady named May from the DMV."

"Oh my gosh. What did she say? Did she recognize Em? Did she leave a number?"

"That's just it, she didn't say much. She said that she wanted you to meet her tonight at ten at the Java Joe in downtown Franklin."

"What time is it now?" Carson looked down at her watch; it was nine forty-five.

"Shoot! I have fifteen minutes. Hunter and I should be able to make it." She headed to the door.

"You can't tell Hunter."

"What do you mean? He has to know, he's the cop. I need to start trusting him before I lose his trust forever."

"That's just it. She said you had to come alone, or she wouldn't talk at all."

"No no no." Carson pressed the crown of her head against the door. "How am I going to do that?" She looked up at Abby. "He won't let me out of his sight. Plus, I promised him no more secrets."

"That's what I'm here for."

"Yeah, great. What are you going to do?"

"Have faith, girlfriend. He already thinks I'm distraught over Gary. I'll just wail it up some more and suggest that you take me out for a beer. He won't want to be around to crying babes. Believe me, I know."

Carson sucked her inner cheek. "Abby, I don't know."

"Trust me. It'll work." She blew on her knuckles and shined them against her shirt. "I'm a pro."

Eight minutes later, they pulled in front of the coffeehouse.

"See, I told you it'd work like a charm."

"Yeah, it was a little too easy."

"What are you talking about? I'm telling you, guys don't like being around crying females. They don't know how to handle it."

"Most guys, yeah, but Hunter's not like most men. I just don't trust it."

"Just stop worrying and go be Ms. Magnum PI." She shooed her out of the car.

The Java Joe was pretty empty. Carson looked around but didn't spot May in the place. She grabbed a seat on a small worn couch in the corner. A small red candle sat on the table, emitting a miniscule shadow. The swirling sounds of frothed milk hissed in the background. No one would notice them here. The waiter arrived, and she ordered a nonfat decaf white mocha latte. She checked her watch. It was ten o'clock.

At 10:02, the waiter brought her mocha. She stared into her mug then sipped the whip cream off. When Carson looked up, May sat across from her.

"May?" The woman resembled nothing of the spitfire she'd met earlier. Her hair stuck out in wild tuffs. She appeared a few inches smaller. She kept her eye on the front door. "I came alone like you asked." Carson wanted her to relax.

"Good."

"So did you recognize my friend?"

"I think I know who killed her."

"Great. You can tell me all about it down at the station."

Hot coffee splashed onto Carson's hand as she jerked around to face Hunter. He stood there with murder in his eyes and a squirming Abby in his grasp.

Chapter 20

"Hunter, I—" Carson took one look at him and shut up. She felt his eyes burn a hole right through her. The veins in his neck pulsed as he craned his head to the left. This was bad. She focused her attention on Abby. Abby shrugged her shoulders and pinched her face in apology. Some pro she was. "Don't worry. Hunter won't suspect a thing." So much for Abby's great acting skills. Then there was poor May. The woman looked like she was about to croak. Who could blame her? Hunter looked like he wanted to pounce on her.

"May, I—"

"You said you were alone."

"She lied." Carson shot Hunter a nasty look.

She turned her attention back to May. "No, I didn't. I was followed. I'm so sorry. I thought I was being careful. Please. You have to believe me." She kept quiet, watching May.

"Who is this guy?"

"I'm—"

Carson interrupted him, not caring for his tone. "His name is Hunter Reeves, and he's the detective in charge of the case."

"I don't want to talk to no police."

"Hunter is a good man. He'll help you. Hunter will take care of everything. Won't you?"

"You are in no position—"

"Excuse us, May." She struggled to drag Hunter away.

"Look, I know you're mad—"

"Mad is not the half of it."

"I know and I'm sorry. I—"

"What are you sorry about? Sorry you got caught? Sorry I showed up before you got any information that you could keep from me?"

"I wanted to tell you, honest, but I—." She read the disbelief on his face. "It doesn't matter right now. All that matters is that woman over there, and you are scaring her to death. You ought to be ashamed of yourself."

"I ought to be ashamed."

"Yes, look at her. Go on look at her."

"Carson, do not test me right now. You are in no position to give me orders."

"You're right." She wished she could turn back the clock. Wished she had confided in him, and the two of them could be here together as a team instead of enemies.

Carson sighed. "You can be mad at me all you want, but don't take it out on that lady. She's frightened, and right now, she's the only real lead in this case."

"Carson, you don't know that." He brushed his hands through his hair. "But I won't know until I have a chance to sit down and talk to her."

"That's fine, but can we just question her here and not take her down to the station?"

"No."

"But—"

"Carson, I can't do it. I have to take her in and question her. I have to make sure it's by the book. That way, there won't be any questions. Do you understand?"

She remembered the conversation they had about his station being under scrutiny for messing up a case. It was one of the main reasons he hadn't looked closer into Em's case. She knew he was right. They had to take her into the station.

"I'll talk to her and see what I can do."

"Thanks, Carson, but I think I can handle this."

"No, you've already scared her once. I'll talk to her."

"Carson, stay put." He left her and sat down next to May. Carson watched him say something to her. He smiled. She smiled back and swatted her hand at him. Amazing. The guy could work his charms on any woman.

The four of them piled into Hunter's car and headed to the station since he refused to let any of them out of his sight. This time, Carson didn't mind. She grew weary of fighting with the man, plus she was too revved up. Carson fidgeted in her seat. She wanted to get to the station and end this. May said she knew who the killer might be. An image of her blonde little friend popped into her head. A sense of relief filled her. She'd been wrong about him knowing anything, and it was one time she relished being wrong.

The car stopped. They reached the station. All of them got out at the same time. Hunter followed behind them and signed them in. The door buzzed, allowing them to proceed into the station. Hunter stopped in front of a scarred wooden door. Carson swallowed. That was the room she'd been in when they told her about Emily. Hunter opened it and led May inside. Carson preceded her but was stopped at the door by Hunter.

"You not allowed in there."

"She's my witness, and I want to hear what she has to say."

He refused to move. "First of all, she's not your witness because you are not a cop; and second, I can't have civilians in there."

"So that's why you wanted to bring her back here so you could keep me out of the loop. You're unbelievable, you know that. I can't believe you're going to keep me in the dark. After everything I've been through to find this person. You're pathetic, cruel, selfish, demanding, pigheaded, womanizing frog." She ran out of steam.

"Are you finished?"

"Don't forget bullying," Abby jumped in.

"Yeah! That too."

"Now are you finished?"

Carson looked over at Abby. Abby shrugged and nodded yes. "Yeah, I think that covers it." Carson stuck out her chin.

"Great because the ogre that I am planned to let you sit in that room over there." He tilted his head toward the door next to May's room. "And watch the whole procedure from the one-way glass if that's all right with you?"

"Oh." Carson crossed her arms over her chest then put them to the side before finally planting them on her hips. "That would be fine."

"You remember my partner, Gary Norton."

Carson smiled at him. "Of course. It's nice to see you again."

"Norton"—Hunter handed Abby and Carson over to him—"take them both in and make sure they behave themselves."

Abby sat down on a chair, watching Norton while Carson stood with her nose pressed against the glass. Hunter placed a glass of water in front of the fragile May. She took a dainty sip, placed the cup back on the table, and turned her attention to Hunter.

"Tell me about Emily." Carson was amazed at how soothing and unintimidating his voice sounded.

"Well, I only saw her that one time at the DMV. I remembered her because it was a pretty slow day. She was overly nice and glowing."

"Glowing?"

"Yeah, you know when a woman's in love." May looked toward the glass.

"Did she say anything to you?"

May turned back to Hunter. "We didn't talk or nothing, she just sat down and got her picture taken."

"Then what happened?"

"Then she left. I didn't think much of it not until that pretty little thing came in today and showed her license. And I remembered." Her shoulders slumped.

"What did you remember?"

"He's a good boy, he doesn't mean any harm. He's not right in the head, you know?"

"Who, May? Who's not right in the head?" Hunter pressed.

"Wayne." She rubbed her hands together. "He don't have family. He worked there with Ida and me, and well, he used to take a lot of drugs. Well, one night, he took way too many, according to some friends of his and disappeared. We were all worried about him because no one had seen him. Then he shows up two months later, only he's different. He was talking real slow, and he had a bit of a limp. Come to find out he passed out from the drugs and slept for four days, and it caused brain damage. No one had the heart to let him go; so we kept him onto work, doing some odd jobs, mostly janitor-type work." She grabbed the water and took a sip.

Carson wanted to scream. What did any of this have to do with Emily? Her hopes of May being any help dwindled in her mind. She sighed but kept staring through the glass as May began to talk once again.

"He was there that day the pretty girl came in. He was mesmerized by her. In fact, he'd never gotten worked up about any girls not since before his little accident."

"Mesmerized, how?" Hunter asked.

"Well, he stopped working and just stared at her. Then he offered to walk her to her car. She knew he wasn't right off the bat, and she was sweet as she could be. She said she'd be honored to have him walk her to her car. He escorted her out, and I watched them talk for a minute. Then he ran back in and started talking about how they were going to go on a date. I let him talk, didn't think nothing about it until today."

"Why?"

"About two days after she got her license, Wayne was in, and he was upset. There were files all over the place, and he was just crazy unlike anything I'd seen. When we finally got him calmed down, he said that Emily had lied to him that she didn't want to take him out. I was confused, and I asked him who Emily was. He told me she was the pretty girl from the other day. Then I asked him how he knew that she didn't want to go on a date. He tells me that he wrote down her address that day from the paperwork and went to her house. And then he said . . ." She paused.

"What did he say, May?"

"He . . . he said he'd make her sorry that she tricked him like that." Tears trickled down her face.

"May, I need his address."

She nodded. "I brought it."

Carson watched her dig a piece of paper from her purse and slide it across the desk to Hunter. She jumped when she felt Abby's hand on her shoulder.

"Car, are you going to be okay?"

She bit her lower lip and nodded. "I can't believe this. She was at the wrong place at the wrong time. She didn't have to die." Her body shook.

"Oh, Car, I'm sorry." Abby embraced her.

Hunter walked through the door and kept his eyes on Carson while he spoke to his partner. "Norton, we need to get a warrant, now."

"It's already being worked out."

"Good." He went to Carson.

"Carson, are you all—"

She flung herself in his arms. "Oh god, Hunter, I can't believe it." She looked up at him and wiped at her tears. "I thought . . . I thought. Damn, I don't know what I thought. But it's so senseless you know. She was being kind and gentle to some half-wit, and it got her killed. Oh god." She clung to him.

"Shh, shh. It's okay." Hunter rubbed her back

"And I'm so sorry for lying about meeting May." Carson pulled back to stare into his face.

He brushed her hair from her face. "We'll deal with that later."

"Um . . . Hunter, the warrant will be ready in a half hour," Gary interrupted.

Hunter let Carson go and nodded to his partner.

Carson suddenly felt cold. Her mind willed Hunter to take her back in his arms. "Hunter—"

"I'm going to go get this guy, okay. And I'm going to have Norton take you and Abby home, all right?"

She wiped her face with the back of her hand. "That's fine. I'll be fine. Thank you."

Abby grabbed hold of Carson's hand, and they began to follow Norton out the door. Carson stopped in the doorway and turned back.

"Be careful, okay."

"Don't worry, you won't get rid of me that easy."

Carson nodded and left.

Chapter 21

Carson peered through the one-way glass into the empty room. Where were they? She paced the room then sat in the wooden chair; within a minute, she jumped back up and resumed pacing. Her mental being wouldn't be able to take much more waiting. Emily's killer still hadn't confessed even after a night behind bars. But Hunter seemed convinced he'd crack any time, and she'd be there to witness his confession. Then this whole nightmare would be over, and Hunter would be out of her life. The door to her room opened; and Gary, Hunter's partner, walked in.

"We're bringing him down the hall now."

Right then, the door to the other room opened; and there he was, Em's killer, followed by Hunter. Carson pressed her hands against the glass. She wanted to throw up. That man was the last vision Emily saw. Oh god, her poor best friend. He looked oily. His long brown hair hung in his eyes and to the middle of his back. He couldn't have weighed more than one hundred and fifty pounds. She glimpsed dirt under his fingernails. His worn, ratty jeans had holes at the knees. She bet anything, the jeans hadn't been washed in the past month. They had that dirty look. The once-white T-shirt under the flannel was a gray color. She closed her eyes and leaned her head against the glass. The memory of his appearance etched into her mind.

She jumped as did Wayne when Hunter slammed his fist against the table.

"Okay, Wayne, let's go over this one more time. We know you had the hots for Emily, we know you followed her home, we know she rejected you, and we know that made you mad enough to want to hurt her. Now let's make this easy on everybody and tell us what happened that night."

"I . . . I . . . I di-di-didn't k-k-kill her."

"Come on, Wayne. I bet it made you feel so good"—Hunter got in his face, forcing Wayne to pull away—"knowing you were the one with the power as you held her head under the water and watched her die."

"N-n-n-no." Wayne shook his head franticly. "No."

"Why didn't you just forget her, Wayne? Why did you kill such a beautiful girl?"

"No!" Wayne rocked back and forth, tears streaming down his face.

Carson wiped a tear off her face. It was awful. She didn't know how much more of this she could take. Five more minutes eked by, and Wayne withdrew more into himself. He rocked harder, a weird mewling sound escaping his mouth. The temperature in Carson's room seemed to raise a hundred degrees. She bolted for the door, needing to get out of there. Gary went after her.

"Carson?"

"I'm sorry, I have to get out of here. Tell Hunter I went home. Good-bye." She ran.

Carson meant to go straight home but instead found herself at the lake. The image of Wayne looking like a broken boy not matching the one of a cold-blooded killer haunted her. She inhaled three deep breaths. The cool air filled her lungs, exhilarating her body. She twisted her neck left then right then took another breath of air before she sprinted along the lake. Freedom smelled so good. Tears fell harder as her strides grew faster.

Had Wayne finally broken and confessed, or had Hunter just broken what little was left of the man inside? Hunter, he had been so ruthless, cold, and frightening. Carson now knew why he was the best. She wouldn't have lasted one second with Hunter. She guessed, probably, not too many guilty people could withstand that drilling. But Wayne had lasted overnight and that morning. Her run trickled to a slow walk. Did that make him innocent or that disturbed? The sweat on her body began to dry, which brought a chill to her system.

What if they were wrong? No, she wiped the thought from her mind. He had to be guilty because the alternative meant she could still be in danger and so could her blond cherub. No, Wayne being the killer was a much better scenario. But—

No no no, she couldn't think like that. At least she kept her thoughts about the boy to herself. He'd be safe. Especially if she just forgot all about him and never came to look for him. She'd never be able to live with herself if he were harmed in anyway. But she didn't have to worry because they had the killer, right? Then why did she feel so uneasy?

She picked up her pace, and the slow jog became a run into a sprint. A stitch pierced her left side. She doubled over, trying to get her breath back to normal. After a minute, she stood back up and walked in a circle.

"Car?"

She jumped at the sound of her name. Off to the left of the path stood her little blond friend.

"Hi." She moved closer. "You remembered my name. But I don't know your name."

"Daniel."

"Hello, Daniel. You seem to spend a lot of time here. Do you ever walk along here at night?" *Stop it, Carson. Walk away and forget this boy. Hunter has the killer in custody.*

"Not anymore. It's spooky at dark time."

"I bet it is. What made you stop coming? Did you see something? Did you see someone get hurt?" What was she doing? She couldn't stop the questions.

"You sure ask a lot of questions."

"I guess that's boring, huh?"

"Do you want to play with me?"

No. Leave him alone. Hunter had the killer now. "I'd love to play with you."

"Come on." His little hand grabbed hers, and he guided her into the woods. "Let's play hide-and-seek. But you can't hide in the water. Okay?"

Carson stopped. "Why?"

"Because bad things happen in the water."

"What bad things?"

"The water monster." He placed his hands on his hips. "Gosh, don't you know anything?"

She knelt down in front of him and softly grasped him by the arms. "Actually, I don't know about the water monster. Can you tell me about him?" Her heart felt like it was in her gut.

"My mom says he's big and scary and takes people under the water and makes them live there, and they never see their mommies and daddies again."

"Your mom?"

He nodded. "That's what took that lady."

"What lady?" Her heart beat faster.

He shrugged his shoulders. "The lady that looks like you."

Carson reeled on her heels. How many times had someone asked her or Emily if they were sisters, too many. She braced herself for the next question.

"Daniel, this is really important. So listen to me, okay?"

He nodded.

"Did your mommy tell you about the lady like me or did you see the monster took her?"

Daniel looked down at his feet. The toe of his right shoe skimmed across the dead leaves and branches.

His reluctance to answer swamped her senses. Was she right? Had he seen everything? She wanted to take this precious angel and hide him away.

"He's really big like a giant. Can we play now?" He peered up at her.

"When you say giant, do you mean big like me?" Wayne flashed into her mind. She hadn't stood next to him, but she gathered he may have been about an inch or two taller than her.

"No, silly. You don't look like a giant. Let's play." He grew impatient.

Oh god, Wayne wasn't the killer. Carson needed to get this boy to the station and to Hunter.

"Daniel." The screech came from behind her. She looked over her shoulder at the five-foot-nothing, ninety-pound blonde Barbie climbing up the path.

Carson turned back to Daniel. "Did you see this giant take that girl into the lake?"

She read the indecision in his eyes. He glanced over her shoulder toward his mom and then back to her.

"Daniel?" She was running out of time.

She watched him open his mouth; then she was eating dirt.

"Get away from my son."

Spitting out dirt, Carson got to her knees and looked up. Barbie may look like a sparrow, but she hit like a defensive lineman.

"Ma'am, I'm not here to hurt your son." Carson got up.

"I've read about sick people like you. Luring little kids away from their home only to kidnap them and kill them."

"Give me a break, lady. Do I look like I'd kill an innocent child?" She brushed the dirt from her hair.

"That's what they said about Ted Bundy?" She pushed Daniel behind her.

She did have a point there. "Listen, I only wanted to talk to him. I need—"

"It's you. You're the one who was trying to break into my house."

So it wasn't the old lady that had called the police. It was her. At least she knew where Daniel lived now.

"Please let me explain."

"Stay back." She pulled a can of Mace from her pocket.

"Okay, okay." Carson placed her hands up. "But we both know what Daniel saw that night."

"I don't know what you're talking about."

"I know this detective, he'll keep Daniel safe. Please."

Barbie maneuvered Daniel and herself toward the path. "Just stay away from me and my son." She ran down the path, pulling Daniel behind her.

Carson watched them leave. Daniel looked back just before he fell from sight. And nodded.

Chapter 22

Frustrated, exhausted, and broken, Carson limped to the mailbox. She picked up yesterday's mail. The pile of junk and catalogs stung against her scrapped hands. Damn, that woman sure knew how to blindside a person. She pictured Daniel's nod as he stepped out of sight. Did that mean yes to her question, or was he saying good-bye? There had to be a way to get to him without Kung Fu Barbie finding out. No, she needed to get to the station and talk to Hunter. But first, she wanted to get cleaned up.

She stopped at the edge of the steps when she spotted the big box perched in front of her door. It couldn't be hers. She hadn't shopped off the QVC channel in months.

Carson squatted down and searched for the label. Her mail slipped from her fingers when she found the box addressed to Emily.

Scooping up her mail, she opened her door and dragged the box into her apartment.

She ripped at the masking tape to no avail. She grabbed a knife and tore through the tape then pulled open the box's flaps. A letter sat atop the contents.

Hey, Cherry,

Dudette, don't know where you've been. Figured you might want your stuff. I didn't ship your board. I found this address, hope it's yours. But I do know you need to get back here because the waves are extreme. And Ham's been totally missing you. I know you're just friends, and you have that dude back home, but you have to admit, Ham's puppy-dog cute. Aloha.

Stacy

Carson read the letter a second time. Her best friend had a guy named Ham chasing after her. She shook herself and wondered if she would have even known her friend if she were still alive.

One thing was certain. Emily came back here to be with this mystery guy just as she suspected. And ten to one, he was the killer, not Wayne. Hunter needed to be called, she knew; but first, she had to look through Em's things.

She put the letter aside then dug into the box. She pulled out some leis, a coconut, a couple of bikinis, sarongs, some T-shirts and shorts, a ribbon, and Em's high school yearbook. What was she carrying this around for? Carson couldn't even remember if she still had hers. She opened up the book then shut it. Now was not the time to reminisce about adolescent hell.

She pushed the book aside and dug back into the box. There were three rolls of film and a framed picture of Emily and three other surfers holding their boards. Well, now she knew why they called him Ham, and he was puppy-dog cute in a Samoan kind of way. She dumped the clothes back into the box. Her fingers skimmed over the framed picture. Emily's smile outshined her companions. She radiated happiness.

"Oh, Em, what happened?" She laid the picture aside. "I wonder what I'll find on these." She scooped up the rolls of film, headed toward the door, stopped, and stared at the phone. She'd call him as soon as she got the pictures developed.

She hit Target first, only to be told that their one-hour photo machine broke. And the local drugstore had closed for remodeling; that left her with no choice but to head to the overcrowded Super Wal-Mart.

The one-hour photo was a little behind. It'd be closer to two hours for her pictures. She left them.

Carson decided to kill time next door at Starbucks. She ordered her usual—decaf, nonfat, sugar-free caramel macchiato with no vanilla, added with whip cream—and took a seat on the patio. She opened the cup to scoop out all the whip cream and eat it before it melted in the coffee.

A young couple sat at the table in front of her. She watched the lovers holding hands while smiling into each other's eyes.

It brought Hunter to the forefront of her mind. What would it be like to share coffee with the man and actually have a conversation? Could they be as happy as that couple? Carson pushed the crazy notions from her mind.

She wondered if he still had Wayne in the interrogation room. She'd call him, she promised herself, once the pictures were in hand.

"Carson?"

Carson looked up at Teddy towering over her table like a giant. She felt her eyes grow like saucers. "Teddy, what are you doing here?"

"I'm in town visiting my parents. Are you okay? You look like you just saw a ghost."

"No, I . . . I guess you just startled me."

"You did seem a million miles away." He looked around then whispered. "Um, how's your investigation going?"

"It's going. Sit down and I'll fill you in."

"No, I can't stay."

"Teddy, are you all right? You seem kind of antsy." The man couldn't keep eye contact with her. He looked as if he'd jump out of his skin at any moment. It was as if he expected someone to catch him talking to her.

"I'm fine. So tell me about the search."

"Well, Hunter, that cop I was telling you about, he has someone in custody now."

"Oh my god."

Carson shook her head. "I know."

"Who is he? Do you know him? Do I know him? When and how did they get him?"

"Whoa, which question should I answer first?"

Teddy looked around then bent down within earshot. "I guess I still can't believe it. I mean, I believed you believed she was murdered, but I couldn't bring myself to accept that fact and now—" He sighed.

"I know." She patted Teddy's hand.

"Teddy." He jumped away from Carson as though she had the plague. Then they both turned their heads toward the sultry voice.

Carson watched the leggy redhead carrying a to-go box with four coffees saunter toward their table. She recognized the woman from the photos on Teddy's mantel. She wondered what Emily would think about Teddy's soon-to-be wife.

"Melinda, here, I'll take those." He grabbed the coffee from her hands. "Mel, honey, this is Carson, a friend of mine from high school."

"Nice to meet you." Melinda held out a perfectly manicured hand.

"You too." Carson felt embarrassed holding out her chipped, broken, unpolished one.

"I hope I didn't disrupt anything."

"Not at all, honey."

Melinda rose one eyebrow. "You two seemed really engrossed in conversation."

"No." He pecked her on her cheek. "We were just catching up on old times. It's been—gosh, how long would you say it's been since we've seen each other? About ten years, right, Carson?"

It was just last week.

Carson choked on her coffee before she looked up at Teddy. She knew her face registered disbelief, and it was too late to change it, but she half-smiled anyway.

"Well, we better get going. Don't want the coffee to get cold. Carson, why don't you send your address to my mom so she can send you an invitation to the wedding."

"Nice to have met you, Carson."

Carson watched the two of them drive off. He lied to his fiancée about their meeting, but why? Unless he had something to hide. Oh god, had he still harbored feelings for Emily and killed her? No, he was marrying a beautiful woman; and truth be told, one much prettier than Emily. No, he couldn't be the killer; he would have taken care of her that night, right? She needed to talk to Hunter and find out if Wayne had broken yet, but deep down, she knew he wouldn't. He wasn't Emily's killer, Carson knew it in her heart.

Curiosity ate at Carson. She paced her small living/dining combo area, her eyes never wavering from the sealed pictures that sat on her table.

Where was that stupid man? She decided she'd work alongside Hunter and no longer try this on her own. Therefore, she refused to open up Emily's pictures she just developed. But the blasted man hadn't returned, nor had he left a message saying when he'd be home.

What was he doing? She called his office only to be told that he wasn't in. She asked to speak to Gary, but he wasn't available either. She also asked about Wayne, but they wouldn't give away any information. And they refused to give her his cell phone number, something about it being illegal to give out that type of information. Hunter had given it to her once, but she ripped up that card when he first refused to help her. She even called BJ, hoping he had the number, but he was unreachable.

She ceased pacing and stared down at the sealed package. What did it matter if she opened the pictures? They had the killer, so these wouldn't be evidence.

Picking up the pictures, she walked to the couch, sat down, and tore open the package. The first two rolls consisted of Emily's time in Hawaii. A couple of pictures showed her hugging different people. She put those ones aside.

She opened the last set, scanning the contents. Her hand slowed and trembled halfway through the pictures.

"Oh my god, oh my god." She felt sick.

The unexpected knock at the door caused her to fling the pictures in the air, scattering them across the floor.

"Just a minute," she called out as she got on her knees to pick up the photos.

"Car?"

She screamed at the sound of BJ's voice. Clutching the pictures to her chest, she looked up at him standing over her.

"Carson, is everything okay?"

"I'm fine. What are you doing here?" She stood up, her death grip tightened on the pictures.

"I got your message, and I was close by, so I came over." He moved closer, and she moved back.

"You could have just called."

He quirked an eyebrow. "I guess you're right, but since I'm here, what's up?"

"Nothing, I'm actually getting ready to leave."

"Car, what the hell is going on? You act like you're afraid of me."

"Afraid of you." She snorted. "That's absurd."

"Really?" He inched closer, and she retreated. "Then why are you backing away from me?" He moved even closer.

She tried to stand her ground but lost. "BJ, I . . . u—"

"This is about last night, isn't it? About the way I lost control and let my anger get the better of me? I thought we got past this, and that you forgave me."

"I—" A picture slipped from her grasp and fell to the floor.

BJ bent down to retrieve it. "What's this?"

He looked up at her.

Carson witnessed his astonished look before she bashed the lamp against his head, sending him crashing to the floor.

"What the—"

She looked over at Hunter framed in the open door. The lamp rolled from her hands. "I think I killed him."

Chapter 23

Like a baby bird learning to fly, Carson fluttered her hands around her face.

"Oh god, what have I done? What have I done? Oh god, BJ, I'm sorry." Tears pricked the back of her eyes as she watched Hunter kneel down and press his two fingers against BJ's neck, looking for a pulse she knew didn't exist. She killed a man. Not just any man, but someone she considered a dear friend. She grabbed the empty cereal bowl off the table and puked.

"He's not dead."

"What?" She stared down at BJ's unmoving body.

"He's not dead, but he's sure gonna have one hell of a headache." He stood up. "Now would you mind telling me what the hell is going on?"

BJ moaned.

Hunter crouched back to him. "BJ, can you hear me? Open your eyes."

"Head, oooh," BJ moaned.

Hunter stared up at her. Concern etched his features. "I'm going to need your help."

Uncertain, her legs carried her over to Hunter. "What do you need me to do?"

"I need you to"—he looked at her then wrinkled his nose—"um, dump out that bowl."

"Bowl." BJ wasn't dead. She looked down at the murky liquid. A fresh wave of nausea threatened to overtake her, but she tamped it down.

Her head began to pound. She wanted to crawl into bed and start the day over.

"Carson, are you listening to me? Carson."

She closed her eyes. Focus. She needed to focus. When she reopened her eyes, Hunter stood before her with BJ slung over his shoulder.

"Go get a towel, fill it with ice. I'm going to put him down on your bed. And then, I want some answers."

When she didn't respond, he got in her face and yelled. "Carson, now!" Then he took BJ to her room.

She hurried to the kitchen, threw the bowl in the sink, then retrieved a dish towel filled with ice and ran to her room.

"Here." She thrust the ice pack in Hunter's face.

She bit her bottom lip when BJ moaned once more as he tried to sit up. He got halfway before he fell back against the pillows.

"Shit." The palms of his hands pressed into his head. He peered at her through one eye. "You tried to kill me." He licked his lips.

"BJ, I—"

"Shhh. Not so loud." He closed his eye. "I guess I can't blame you. I'd probably have done the same thing."

"Would someone tell me what the hell is going on?"

Once again, BJ opened one eye and looked at Carson. "You didn't tell him."

She looked away.

"Tell me what?"

"Carson thinks I murdered Emily."

Her head whipped around, and they made eye contact.

"What?" Hunter barked. "I have the killer in custody."

BJ took his eyes off Carson and looked at Hunter. "Did you just say you have the killer?"

"Yes."

"No," Carson replied simultaneously with Hunter's yes.

They both stared at her.

"Carson, what the hell's the matter with you?" Hunter questioned.

"I don't think Wayne is the killer."

"Carson, he's the killer."

"Who's Wayne?" BJ tried to sit up.

"I don't think he is."

"Carson." Hunter rubbed his eyes.

"Did he confess yet?"

Hunter stopped. "No, but he will."

"He won't." Carson folded her arms across her chest.

"Would someone tell me what's going on?"

"Let me get this straight, you don't think Wayne's the killer because you believe he"—Hunter pointed to BJ—"a man who, you told me yesterday, was a gentleman and who you've known forever is the killer."

"I . . . yes . . . um . . . no . . . I don't know, it's just I found this . . . um . . . well, it's . . . um . . . Let me just go get it." She started to leave.

"Um, Carson, if you don't mind, I'd rather we kept that to ourselves."

"Keep what to yourself?" Hunter demanded.

She knew her face turned crimson, the picture, vivid in her mind. BJ lay completely naked in all his masculine glory upon silk sheets. A blindfold draped his eyes while his hands were tied to the bedposts; an anticipating grin etched on his features. Carson remembered the shock on his face when he picked up the picture. He definitely didn't know it ever existed. Unable to stop herself, her eyes strayed to a certain part of his body.

"Someone's going to tell me what's going on?"

Carson flinched, feeling the color deepen on her cheeks. Hunter stood, arms crossed, glaring at her, while BJ gave her a sly smile. Her anger got the better of her.

"What was I supposed to think?"

"You could have asked questions first and bashed my head later. You could have trusted me, Carson."

"Like you trusted me?" The guilt she saw reflected in his eyes was all the proof she needed that he truly hadn't trusted her. The knowledge wounded her deep.

"How could you sit here in my house and offer to help me find Emily's killer and keep the fact that you were sleeping with her a secret."

"You were what?" Hunter uncrossed his arms.

Ignoring Hunter, BJ kept his attention on Carson. "I wanted to tell you a million times. I just . . . It had nothing to do with the case."

"I beg to differ."

"Cut the shit, Hunter. Do you really think I killed her? That in a fit of jealous rage, I offed her because she didn't love me."

"She had to have loved you," Carson spoke.

"No, Carson, she didn't love me." He stared hard at her. "It was sex, pure and simple."

"That's a lie. Emily wasn't like that. She didn't sleep around. I know her better than anybody."

"Carson, that's why I didn't tell you." He rubbed the knot on his forehead. "You always thought she was better than you. You placed Emily on this pedestal as though she was an angel. I didn't want to take that away from you."

"No."

"Carson, if she truly loved me, then why didn't she tell you about me?"

"Because you probably used her like you do all your women." Her fury rose at the thought of Emily being one of his conquests.

"I bet she felt used. God, she must have been humiliated. She also knew if she told me, I'd go after you and kick your ass."

"God, you are stubborn. She didn't tell you because, in some sick way, she loved that you cherished her so much, and she didn't want that to change."

"No, Emily would have told me you hit on her."

"Carson, I didn't hit on Emily. Emily came to me. We had an arrangement."

"What kind of arrangement? When was the last time you saw her? Did you sleep with her that last time?"

"Wow, Carson you're learning. I'm proud of you." BJ smiled.

"Oh my god. That's why you didn't believe me at first about her being murdered. You actually thought she'd gotten drunk and jumped into the lake. What aren't you telling me? What else about Emily don't I know?"

"Car, there's nothing else. But I never meant to hurt you, and I didn't kill her."

"I know you didn't kill her, but this changes everything." She sighed.

"It changes nothing, Carson. Wayne is our only suspect," Hunter said.

"Would someone tell me who Wayne is?"

"You"—Hunter turned on BJ—"I ought to haul you in for obstruction of justice. If I didn't have this suspect, you'd bet your ass I'd haul you down to the station and make you a prime suspect."

"Yeah, I'd like to see you try." BJ snorted.

Hunter got in his face. "Maybe Carson's right. Maybe I do have the wrong killer. Maybe I should investigate you."

Carson watched the two of them, and she wanted to scream. They were like little boys fighting over a toy. She'd never seen two men hate each other so much, and she wondered about it.

"Stop it, both of you, I've had it."

"Carson, stay out of this," Hunter warned.

"Okay. Let's do it. Haul me down to the station and press charges. I'll just use my one phone call to call my attorney. I wonder what Uncle Harold would say about his own son trying to pin a murder on his cousin."

Chapter 24

Cousins. With squinted eyes, she looked from one to the other. Where Hunter was tall, blond, and blue-eyed, BJ was a tad shorter with dark hair and gray eyes. No two men looked further apart. Yet they were both in crime-solving careers. Some of their mannerisms were the same, like their macho take-charge attitudes. And they were both really good with women, too good. Then the enormity of the situation hit her hard. They were cousins, flesh and blood, and neither one bothered to fill her in on that information. Why hadn't they told her? Why the big secret? And how could she have known BJ for the past ten years and never once come in contact with Hunter?

"Get out." Her finger pointed toward the door. "Both of you get out of my house right now."

"Carson," BJ moaned.

"Don't you think you're being a little emotional?" Hunter piped in.

"You are both lying, manipulative jerks." She planted her hands on her hips. "And you"—her full ire on BJ—"have lied to me twice."

"I didn't lie to you."

"You . . ." He had a point. "You lied by omission. I can't believe you kept this from me."

"It wasn't important." He grabbed his head.

"Well, it's important to me." Some of the fight left her when she saw how much pain he was in, and she had been the cause.

"Why? It doesn't mean anything. We're related by blood, but we stopped being cousins years ago."

Hunter looked bored. That excited her anger further. The man was a cad. The fact that he (a) didn't tell her they were cousins, (b) almost started a fight with him the night before, and (c) was looking at her as though she were a child throwing a tantrum proved that she could never have this man in her life. Crime solving and *sex* were the only things he cared about. If he didn't even care for his own flesh and blood, how could he ever care for her? Reality hit her right in the solar plexus. Unless she was willing to have mad, passionate, no-strings-attached sex, she'd never have this man.

"I want you both out of here in twenty minutes."

"Can't do that, darling. I live here remember?"

"And I . . ." BJ moaned a shade too dramatically.

"You what?" BJ sat up as he looked from Hunter to Carson.

"You heard me. I live here."

"Carson?"

"Not by my choice." Carson rubbed her hands across her eyes. "But that's about to change. I want you both gone."

"I'm not going anywhere." Hunter leaned against the bedpost.

"Actually, you are. Since there's no longer a killer on the loose, you no longer need to be here. So get out and take your cousin with you."

"I doubt I'm fit to get out of this bed." BJ leaned back against the pillows.

"And if I recall a few minutes ago, you told me you didn't think Wayne was the killer, and if you're right and I left you alone and something happened to you, I'd have failed. So I think it'd be wise if I stayed until I got a confession out of Wayne."

Carson looked at both of them. "Fine. Stay here. You both can kill each other for all I care. I'll be staying the night at Jamie's."

Carson halted just outside the door and almost charged back inside when she heard their arguing voices. Good sense and weariness prevailed. They could beat the snot out of each other for all she cared. She turned her back to the noise, tuning it out.

She surveyed the mess in her living room. Pictures littered the floor, the lampshade lie atop of the photos, and her one and only lamp was bent. She picked it up and turned it sideways. BJ was lucky to be alive. Goose bumps raised on her flesh at the thought of how she almost killed him. What possessed her to think that BJ murdered Emily? Fear and uncertainty along with the way he had acted the night before. He'd been so angry that his eyes held the look of someone capable of deadly harm.

Nothing was as it seemed, and she didn't know what to make of any of it. BJ and Emily had been lovers. Was that why he didn't believe she'd been murdered at the beginning? Had he known a different side of Emily that made him suspect she could get drunk and drown herself? It definitely made sense when he had told her that people weren't always what they seemed. A part of her wished she had taken his advice and left this case alone. Then again, she'd never be able to live with herself if she'd sat and done nothing.

Which meant she needed to find some way to put her sensibilities aside and go back into her room and work with the testosterone twins. Cousins, she still couldn't believe it. And she wondered what had happened between the two of them to make them hate each other. There was no doubt about the hatred that radiated around them. Had they fallen in love with the same woman and gotten burned? The thought of either of them so in love with a woman that it could end family ties curdled her stomach. Oh crap, this was getting too complicated. Did she really want to know? No. Yes. Oh, all she wanted was her life back, but she knew it'd never be the same.

She sighed then sucked in a deep breath, preparing herself to enter the war zone.

Before she made it to the room, a knock on the door halted her progress.

Good, a reprieve from dealing with the two of them. She headed to the door and answered it.

"Mrs. J."

"Carson." Mrs. J strode past her, a dull-dead look in her eyes.

Carson closed the door and met her in the living room. Like a child about to be scolded, she placed her hands behind her back and rocked on the balls of her feet.

"Can I get you something to drink?"

"This isn't a social call, Carson." A tear streaked down her cheek.

"Mrs. J, what's . . ." She moved closer.

"How could you, Carson?"

The steel sound of her voice caused Carson to slow to a stop. "Mrs. J, what did I do?"

"Just stop it. Teddy came to see me, and he told me everything. Is it true?"

Carson closed her eyes and sighed. Teddy. How could she have completely forgotten about him? "What exactly did Teddy tell you?"

"You know what he told me. How could you do this to us? I asked you to let it go." She wrung her hands.

"Mrs. J." Carson tried to place an arm around her in comfort, but she rebuffed the move. It cut Carson to the quick. "Mrs. J, I'd think you'd be happy to know that we got the person who did this to Em."

"You thought I'd be happy to relive Em's death all over again. You thought I'd be happy to know that some sick stranger murdered my baby."

"So you'd rather let her name be tarnished. Let people think she was some drunk who drowned herself."

"What?" Mrs. J's eyes looked like saucers.

"Yes, Mrs. J, I know all about you trying to put Emily into rehab, and that was the reason she ran off to Hawaii or California or wherever she went."

"We brought you into our home, treated you like family, and you do this. You stab me in the back. For what? To prove that you were right?" Her voice rose a few octaves.

"Mrs. J, it's not like that."

"Is this a case of classical jealousy, Carson?"

"What?" The question, a whispered breath.

"You always were jealous of Emily. Wishing we were your family, always wearing her clothes instead of the hand-me-downs your parents scrounged up. But you were never as good as her, and you never will be."

Carson held on to the back of a chair, her eyes stared at the couch, refusing to meet the woman's hateful gaze. Mrs. Johnson's cruel words sliced into her soul inch by inch.

"That's where you're wrong."

Carson jerked up her head, her eyes connecting with Hunter. How long had he been there? Had he heard Mrs. J's comments and would he believe them?

"Detective Reeves." Mrs. Johnson clutched her hand to her collar. "How long have you been standing there?"

"Long enough to know you are way out of line."

Carson looked away. Hunter's defense of her warmed her heart. And she could almost forgive him for being a lying cad.

"Mrs. Johnson. I know how hard this must be for you. Losing your only child, but I also think in time you'll be glad the truth came out." He had moved to stand next to Carson. "And if not for Carson's persistence, this could have gone unnoticed, and the guy could have killed again."

"Carson's persistence? Just how persistent was she, Detective?"

Carson gasped.

"You are way out of line, lady," Hunter yelled.

She backed up. "What would your boss think if he knew you slept with witnesses. And as for you"—her full attention geared to Carson—"it should have been you that died." Mrs. J curled her lip. "I never want to see you again." She stormed out of the apartment.

The slamming of the door vibrated through the apartment.

"Carson." Hunter placed a hand on her shoulder.

"Don't, I'm fine." She cringed away from his touch.

"She's just hurting right now. You know she didn't mean a word she said."

"Hunter, I said I was fine." She kept her back to him. "I believe we have work to do."

Chapter 25

On the verge, out of control, *snap*. That's how Carson felt. That she'd snap at any moment, and there'd be no turning back. Who was she kidding? She already passed that point, and she passed it with Mrs. J. She clamped one hand over her ears to block the hateful words Mrs. Johnson spewed at her.

"I wished it were you they found in that lake."

And there it was. Mrs. J didn't hate her because she forced the issue of Em's death. She hated her because she still lived while her one and only daughter lay dead. And Carson understood that—kinda.

It took all her energy not to run down to the nearest bar and drink the image of Mrs. J's hate for her from her mind. Then there was Hunter; pity marring his handsome features, wanting her to talk about it, cleanse her system. Why didn't he just take out his gun, shoot her in the gut, then throw salt on the wound.

She had checked the rearview mirror a dozen times after she left, expecting to see Hunter behind her with his flashing red lights. But for once, he had finally listened to her and let her go off alone.

Alone. Cold air penetrated the inside of her car. She sighed, watching her breath. An icy frost began to cover the windshield. Jesus. How long had she been here? And why? Because she had wasted too much time already. It was time to take control and end this sordid mess. Or at least, get some answers.

She clapped then rubbed her cold hands together before exiting her car. After she closed the door, she stared at the house that loomed before her.

They were home. A light shone from the left side of the house, possibly from the kitchen.

She steeled herself for the confrontation and forged her way up the stairs to the front door. No time for niceties, she beat on the door. Within a minute it opened.

"Car."

"Hi, Daniel." She looked down at the little boy.

"May I come in?" He stepped back and let Carson enter the foyer.

"Daniel, honey, don't answer the door without Mommie." Barbie Doll strolled down the hallway, wearing a checkered apron with a silver mixing bowl in one hand and a wooden stirring spoon in the other. Her blond hair was a tangled mess atop her head, and flour stuck to her nose. Carson didn't think it possible, but she looked more beautiful than she did earlier at the lake. A warm glow and contented smile filled her face until she looked up from her bowl and found Carson standing inside her house.

"You. Get out of my house before I call the police."

"No, Mom, Car's my friend; and she came to see me and play with me. Right?" His blue eyes looked up at Carson.

"Daniel, go to your room, now."

"Gosh, Mom, you never let me have any friends anymore. I can't even go to school. I wish Dad were here. I wish it were you—" He burst from the room.

"Daniel . . . ," his mother called after him.

"We need to talk," Carson spoke.

"Save it for the police when they take you to jail for breaking and entering." She headed toward the phone on the entry hall table.

"Daniel, let me in."

"Huh." She had the receiver in her hand.

"Go ahead, call the police. That will save me a lot of time. I can tell them how Daniel witnessed the murder of the woman at the lake."

Barbie's dainty hand stopped dialing. "They won't believe you." She proceeded to start dialing.

"Are you willing to take that chance?"

Barbie slammed down the phone.

"I'm not trying to hurt you. I only want to help." Carson assured her.

"We don't need your help."

"Really? Then why have you cut Daniel off from his friends and school? That isn't healthy for—how old is he, five?"

"He's almost nine." She shook from head to toe.

"Nine, but he's so—"

"Small. I know. He was born two months premature and spent the first three months of his life in a hospital. I prayed every night that my son would live, that I'd see him grow up." She took in a deep breath. "I promised to protect him, and that's what I intent to do. So please just leave and forget about us."

Carson hurt for this woman, but it still wasn't enough to stop her from finding answers.

"I can't do that. See, that woman that was killed, she was my best friend."

Barbie stared at her. "I'm sorry, but I don't know what woman you're talking about."

"Yes, you do, but let me refresh your memory. She was a young woman about my age. Look at me." Carson waited for Barbie to look into her eyes. "We look somewhat alike, but no one would be able to tell that from the way she was found. No one would notice that the pale bluish green skin, the bloated body, and the frightened, lifeless blue eyes once belonged to a beautiful person."

Barbie jammed her spoon into the bowl. "The police said it was an accident. So you are wasting your time, miss."

"I think you know as well as I do that she was murdered." Barbie averted Carson's stare. She continued. "And I think Daniel may be the key to the killer and so do you." She'd hold off telling her about Wayne; she wanted the woman to admit on her own that Daniel had witnessed Em's murder.

Barbie looked upon her this time. "He's just a little boy."

"A boy who's trapped in this house and sneaks out at night. And who plays and hides in the woods all day. Which makes no sense. You won't let him go to school, but he can skulk around the woods."

"I don't let him hang around the woods. Sometimes when I leave him alone in the backyard, he sneaks down there, but I usually catch him before he gets too far, and other times . . . Besides, I don't have to justify myself to you."

"The other times, where does he go in the woods?"

"I don't know." Her face grew crimson.

"What? A woman was murdered there. And you have no idea where your son goes."

"Look," she belted then quietly continued, "he's got a secret hideaway there." She sighed. "He and his father built a secret fort. Only the two of them know about it. They used to sleep there on the weekends. It was like some big adventure."

Carson felt her patience slip. This woman was a nut job. She forbids her son to go to school but lets him roam around the woods. She closed her eyes and pinched the bridge of her nose with her forefingers. Then she thought of something. If Daniel spent the weekend nights there, now that he wasn't in school, did he sleep there during the week? Carson would bet anything that Daniel had been sleeping there the night Emily was murdered.

She opened her eyes. "When was the last time Daniel and his father stayed there?"

Barbie turned away, but not before Carson saw tears pool in her eyes.

"It's been over a year."

A year. That didn't make sense. "Look, Barbie—"

"Barbie?" Her head snapped back toward Carson.

"Look." Carson snapped her hands, her fingers rigid and at attention. "I need some answers. I don't think you realize what it's like to lose someone you love. So if I can't get any answers from you, then maybe I should speak to your husband."

"You can't. My husband is dead." She advanced on Carson. "So don't talk to me about losing a loved one. I know far better than you that kind of pain."

Carson backed up, relaxing her hands to her side. "I'm sorry. I didn't . . . um . . . know."

"Now would you please go?"

"If you know what I'm going through, then why won't you help me?"

"I've already lost my husband. I'll be damned if I lose my son too." She walked to the front door and held it open. "I'm sorry for your loss. But we can't help you."

"Are you sure Daniel hasn't slept in that hideaway recently?"

A flash of surprise heightened Barbie's eyes; but then in a blink, her stern, self-assured look was back.

"Good night, Ms. O'Hara."

Carson knew she'd get no answers from this woman. She didn't blame the woman for clamming up and, in fact, found herself admiring and liking her even if she looked like she belonged in a Mattel box. But she knew she created some doubt in her mind, and it was time to create some more.

"Don't you think that if someone like me could put two and two together and suspect your son as a witness, then the killer may be onto him too?" Carson hated herself for putting her through this.

The bowl dropped out of her hands. "Get out of my house right now, or this time, I will call the police."

"I'll leave. But—" Carson dug into her purse. "If you change your mind or need to talk to me, here's my card." She placed it on the table then headed out the door.

"Carson."

She spun around, high-held expectations vibrating through her body. "Yes."

"Don't ever show your face here again."

She slammed the door in Carson's face.

Chapter 26

Carson trudged through the door of her apartment. Not sure what to expect, she braced herself for Hunter's onslaught. She'd beat him to the punch.

"Before you say anything—" The words fell silent. The apartment was empty. Yet it wasn't the same mess she'd left.

The pictures had been picked up and placed on the table. The lamp stood in its place, albeit a little crooked. And the smell, something smelled extremely wonderful. She went to the kitchen, and pasta sauce simmered on the stove. Well, Detective Reeves seemed to be handy in the kitchen. Where was he?

She headed to the bedroom and came up short. BJ lay sound asleep on her bed. On tiptoes, she maneuvered herself to the side of the bed closest to him. He slept curled up on his left side. His hand balled into a fist near his face. Besides his partially opened lips, there was no expression on his face. He looked like a little boy without a care in the world. Carson leaned closer and noticed the slight bump on his forehead.

She reached out her left hand to caress away the damage she had inflicted when she heard him sigh as he rolled onto his back.

"Hi." He looked up at her.

"Um, hi." She yanked her hand down to her side.

"Are you okay?" He yawned.

"The question should be 'how are you?'"

He pulled himself upright then plumped the pillows behind his back and leaned against them. "I'll live."

"God, BJ. I am so terribly sorry. I—"

"Hey, come here." He scooted over then patted the side of the bed for her to join him.

Her body refused to move. Her eyes directed to BJ's hand and the spot where he wanted her to sit. What was wrong with her? It was BJ, for goodness' sakes. He was harmless, wasn't he? Or was she hitting unknown waters with no ship to bring her safely back to dry land.

"Carson?"

She pulled herself out of her trance and looked up at BJ, catching his hurtful expression. This was crazy. They were friends, and she knew he had nothing to do with Emily's death. So what, they'd been lovers, but why did it irk her? She sat down.

"I shouldn't have hit you."

"No, you had every right to think what you did. I should have told you. God, I wanted to tell you."

"Why didn't you?"

"I—" He sat up from the pillows then reached out his hand and tucked a stray piece of hair back behind her ear. "It's just, I didn't know how or what to say. You have to believe me when I tell you that I never meant to hurt you or keep this from you." He licked his lips.

Carson licked hers in response. She tried to swallow the lump lodged in her throat. The hand he used to brush her hair away still held her hair. She felt him inch closer. She closed her eyes.

"Carson?" Hunter bellowed.

Her eyes popped open as she jumped off the bed.

BJ moaned then lolled back against the pillows. Carson looked away. Oh god, he'd been about to kiss her. And she almost let him.

She turned to him. "What were you thinking?" she whispered.

"What does it look like? And why are we whispering?"

She checked the door. "You are one of my best friends. You should know better. And—"

"Carson?" Hunter stood in the doorway. He looked from her to BJ and back at her. "What's going on?"

"I wanted to make sure BJ was all right, seeing that I almost killed him." She looked back at BJ and almost balked at the content expression on his face. Alarm bells went off in her head.

She looked back at Hunter. Sniffing the air, she asked, "What's that smell?"

"My sauce." Hunter took off toward the kitchen.

In one jagged motion, she crossed her arms at her chest then jerked her head around to BJ. "How could you?"

"What?"

"You know what? You're supposed to be one of my best friends. You lied to me twice and now this." She still whispered.

"Carson, I have no idea—"

"Don't even. This is about Hunter?"

"Hunter has nothing to do with this."

She ignored him. "I don't know what happened between the two of you to make you such enemies. But I will not be used by you or him in some revenge game."

"You have it all wrong."

"Shut up or I'll go get that lamp and hit you again. I won't be a part of any stupid games you and Hunter play. Our friendship depends on that. Got me?" She left before he could answer.

Dinner was delicious, but it was marred by the hostility that radiated through Hunter and BJ. If the two weren't shoveling pasta down their throat, they were growling at each other, and Carson couldn't look at either of them. She stared down at her food and twirled the pasta on her fork.

"Where did you go tonight?"

Her fork clanked against the china bowl. When she looked up, they both stared at her. "I went to get some fresh air and think." She shrugged.

BJ seemed content with her answer while Hunter looked at her with a strange glint in his eyes.

"You were gone for some time," he questioned.

"Well, sometimes it takes me awhile to think. Besides, I thought the two of you could use the time alone."

"Carson, please tell me where you—" Hunter stared down at the beeper on his belt. He got up from the table and went straight for the phone.

Carson held her breath as she watched him dial the phone.

"This is Reeves . . . what!" He stared at Carson. "Shit, son of a bitch. When? I'll be right there." He hung up then punched the wall.

"What's happened?" Carson felt the pasta rising up her throat.

"Wayne tried to kill himself."

"What?"

"The good news is that he isn't dead. The bad news is that he's in a coma. I have to go."

"I'm coming with you." Carson got up.

"Carson, I don't think that's a good idea."

"Hunter, I'm coming."

"No, you are not." He grabbed her by the arms. "There's nothing you can do there. Besides, it's a crime scene, my captain won't allow you there anyway. When I have more details, I'll call you."

She looked up into his face. "Did he confess before he tried to kill himself?"

"No, but trying to kill himself is pretty much a confession."

"What does that mean?" Carson asked.

"It means you can finally put Emily to rest. You did it, Carson. You brought justice to Emily."

"But he never confessed, which means—"

"Which means nothing. He might not have said the words, but his actions tonight prove that he was most definitely our man."

It felt wrong. Carson needed to tell Hunter about Daniel. "Hunter, there is this little boy—"

"Carson, tell me about it later, I have to go."

"But—"

Hunter ignored her. "And you"—he pointed at BJ—"are coming with me. I'll drop you off at the hospital and have your head looked at."

"I'm fine, and I'm staying."

"No, BJ. Hunter's right. Please just go with him. I'd feel better knowing you were fine." Plus, she wanted to be alone. Wayne, their only suspect was in a coma; and it only brought more fear to Carson, not relief.

Chapter 27

"Carson, you have a phone call."

The knife Carson used to cut limes paused in midair as she looked over her shoulder. "Who is it?"

"I don't know." The eighteen-year-old perky hostess shrugged. "They didn't say."

Carson blew a few stray bangs out of her eyes while she watched the little girl bounce back to the front door. Then she put down the knife and rubbed her lime-pulped hands down her apron. When she reached the desk, two of the lines blinked red.

"Which line?"

"I don't remember." Perky girl giggled.

Carson curled her lip in a fake smile. She wondered if she'd been that dumb at eighteen. Sighing, she picked up the receiver and decided to go with line 1.

"This is Carson." The other line was silent.

"Hello, is anyone there?"

"Is this Carson O'Hara?" a muffled voice asked.

Carson pulled the phone away from her ear and made a face at the receiver.

"Who is this?"

"I . . . um . . ."

"Jack, is that you? You know it's not funny, and I don't have time for games."

"I'm sorry I shouldn't have called."

Carson stared at the dead phone line. After a minute, she hung it up then wandered to the bar. That was truly weird. Instinct said to call Hunter, but common sense said to drop it. It'd been five days since Wayne tried to kill himself. He still hadn't woken from his coma. Although he never confessed, the police believed the fact that he hung himself proved he was their man. No one had bothered to confiscate his belongings. They had figured him too slow to think of suicide. And his suicide attempt made no sense to Carson.

She had witnessed his interrogation. He was adamant about his innocence, and he was scared. She didn't know the man, but she sensed his fear. His fear that no matter how much he protested, he'd never be believed. So in her mind, she felt his attempted suicide was an act of desperation, not guilt. But she was the only one, not even Hunter nor BJ would stick by her this time. It was over, and she had to deal with it or continue to search on her own.

But she didn't want to be on her own. She actually missed Hunter. He tried to call her a few times, but she felt it better to go cold turkey, and she ignored his calls. Her brain knew she's done the right thing, but her heart wished she had answered his calls.

She shook the melancholy thoughts from her mind. That chapter was done, and it was time to start a new one—alone.

Carson grabbed the knife and began to cut limes.

"Gee, Carson, you're popular today. You have another phone call."

The knife missed the lime and nicked Carson's thumb. "Dammit, dammit, dammit." She stuck the finger in her mouth. Grabbing a towel, she wrapped it around her thumb and charged to the phone.

"This is Carson."

"Carson." The muffled voice again.

Carson felt dizzy. "Who wants to know?" She cleared her throat. Silence answered her. Her body jerked from the cold chill across her spine.

"Look, I don't know who you are, but this isn't funny. So please leave me alone."

"Wait, don't hang up."

The muffled voice gave way to a feminine one. "Who are you?"

"I . . . I . . . this is Melinda. I don't know if you remember me. We met last weekend."

"I remember you." How could she forget Teddy's gorgeous fiancée?

"I'm sorry if I scared you. I didn't mean to. I just didn't know who else to call or what to do." She sobbed.

"Is Teddy okay? What's the matter?"

"Teddy's fine."

This was weird. "If it's not Teddy, I don't see how I can help you. I hardly know you."

"I know. I'm sorry. I probably shouldn't have called you, but I'm so scared."

"Scared? Scared of what?" Carson felt the hairs on the back of her neck rise.

"I didn't know who else to call."

"Melinda, tell me what the problem is."

"It's . . . it's . . . um . . . I'm sorry I called. I have to go. Please don't tell anyone that I called you."

Once again, Carson stared at the dead receiver. Carson wasted no time. She punched an outside line and dialed. He answered on the first ring.

"Hunter."

"Carson, what a wonderful surprise. Actually, I was just thinking about you."

"Listen, Hunter, I just had the weirdest phone call from Melinda Brant."

"I don't know her, but if she made you think of me, she's okay in my book."

"This isn't a joke."

"Okay, Carson, what's up? You sound spooked. What did she say to you?"

"It's not what she said, it's what she didn't say. Melinda is Teddy Jackson's fiancée."

"And—"

"And Teddy was the love of Emily's life in high school. This has to do with Em. I just know it."

"Carson." He sighed. "Not this again. It's over. Wayne is our man."

"Then explain the phone call I just got."

"I can't do that because I don't know this person."

Carson wanted to jump through the phone and strangle the stubborn man. Why couldn't he see what she saw?

"She told me she didn't know who else to call and that she was scared. Why would she say that to me? I'm a complete stranger to her. But she knows who Em is and knows I'm her best friend, so it has to be that. Don't you see?" She hated the whine in her voice.

"Carson, what I see is a woman obsessed with another dead woman. I bet you're not sleeping or eating. Am I right?"

She refused to answer him.

"When was the last time you relaxed, had a good night sleep, and relished living?"

"I'm sleeping just fine."

"Car, you're starting to scare me. Emily has taken over your life, and I don't think you'll be satisfied until you join her in the afterlife. I think you should talk to someone."

"I am not crazy, Detective Reeves. I just got a frantic call from a woman who is about to marry my dead best friend's ex-boyfriend. I'm not even a cop, and that sends warning bells off in my head. But I'm sure you don't want to mess up your perfect case record and have your station look stupid again for screwing up." The minute the words tumbled out, she wished she could retrieve them.

"Are you finished?"

She heard the warning in his voice, and she wanted to apologize but she couldn't. This was too important.

"No, I'm not finished. You never met Teddy, but he's a big guy, and I should have seen it earlier. Daniel said that the water monster was a big guy that took the girl that looked like me under the water. He was talking about Teddy and Emily."

"Whoa, whoa. Who's Daniel, and what the hell is a water monster?"

Carson scrunched her eyes closed and tapped her fingers between her eyes.

"Carson?"

"Daniel is a little boy who lives by the lake. I befriended him, and although he hasn't actually admitted it, I know he saw Emily's murder."

"Wait a minute. You may have had a witness, and you never told me about it. Un-fucking-believable."

"I tried to tell you about him. The night Wayne tried to kill himself, but you ignored me. Then it became so frantic and messy with Wayne that it never came up."

"It never came up? Dammit, Carson."

"He's just a little boy, and he lost his father last year, and his mother keeps him hidden. I'm sorry, I just felt too protective of him."

"You're sorry. You're sorry."

"Hunter, I—"

"Don't bother. Where does this boy live?"

"I don't think—"

"Where is the boy?'

"I'll tell you on one condition."

"What?"

"That I take you to him."

"No. Now, where is he?"

"His mother won't let you near him. I go, or you get nothing." Carson hated the silence that hung between them. She pictured his handsome face crimson and his eyes the color of blue fire. She knew he'd give in and take her, but she also knew her latest stunt would cost her.

"I'll meet you at the lake this afternoon."

For the third time that morning, Carson stared into a dead receiver.

Chapter 28

Carson pulled into the parking area. She wondered how long Hunter had been there. He leaned against his car. Sunglasses hiding his aquamarine eyes, his long jean-clad legs crossed at the ankles. She swallowed down the sense of longing he stirred inside of her. Like a child about to be scolded, she got out of her car.

"Hi." She waved. "You look good."

"I wish I could say the same about you."

Carson jerked from the slap in the face.

"You've lost weight, and the circles under you eyes are so dark they look like that pavement over there." He pointed over her shoulder.

"It's nice to see you too, Hunter."

"Carson." He reached out a hand then pulled it back. "Take me to the boy."

They hiked up the back trail in silence, the fresh air doing nothing to cool Hunter's anger. Carson felt winded and frazzled by the time they reached the top while Hunter looked as though he just finished a leisurely lunch. Maybe she did need to start taking better care of herself.

She escorted him to Daniel's front door. She rocked on the balls of her feet while Hunter banged on the door. After a moment, he tried the handle, and the door swung open. Carson stared at Hunter. He looked down at her.

"Stay here." He started inside.

"No way." She was right behind him.

"No." She gasped. The place was empty. She rushed through all the rooms. There was nothing left, not even a roll of toilet paper in the bathrooms. Even so, she continued to scream Daniel's name.

"Carson, they're gone."

She stopped and turned back to look at Hunter. "Oh god, Hunter, what have I done."

"It's not your fault, they moved out."

"Yes, it is. How could I have been so stupid? The night that Wayne attempted suicide I visited them. She wouldn't let me talk to Daniel. She kept saying that he didn't know anything. I got so frustrated. I scared her."

"You scared her? How exactly did you do that?"

She looked down at the floor and shook her head. "I did. I told her that if I was smart enough to link Daniel to the killer, then maybe the killer was onto them too."

"What?"

She had no time to move before Hunter seized both her arms and forced her to look up at him.

"I didn't know what else to do."

"You could have trusted me. I can't believe you were cruel enough to scare a mother like that."

"I wasn't being cruel, I was desperate. I knew he could help us."

"When you use a child like that, it's cruel. I would have never believed you could be that ruthless to get what you want. I truly thought you were different."

"No, you don't understand."

"I understand everything. Good-bye, Carson." He turned away.

"Wait, where are you going?" She hated the desperate sound of her voice. But she knew no other way to stop him from walking out. "Please don't go. I need you."

He stopped and turned back toward her. Her pent-up breath escaped her lungs.

"Carson"—he rubbed his eyes—"that's just it, you don't need me. There's nothing I can do for you."

"How can you say that? I do need you." Oh god, was she actually begging this man to stay?

"No." he shook his blond head. "Since I met you, you've told me how you don't need anyone else. How you can manage all on your own. Now that I've gotten to know you, I finally see that. All you need is yourself and the memories of a dead friend."

"What? After everything we've been through. Hunter, we have something—"

"We never had a chance."

"What are you talking about?"

"You're an enigma. And the death of your best friend is going to be the death of you. I'm sorry we had to meet like this. And I'm sorry you can't let this go, and it's turning you into this person who doesn't care who she hurts. I don't want to know that person."

"But wait. What about Teddy and his fiancée." She grabbed his arm.

"It's over, Carson. All of it. Good-bye." Like a statue, she watched Hunter walk out the door.

Carson reached the car, and the last bit of hope that Hunter may have just been ranting diminished when she found her corvette alone in the parking lot. He had meant it. After weeks of trying to push him away, she'd finally succeeded. And once again, she was alone searching for an unknown killer.

Carson trudged up the stairs to her apartment. With no recollection of driving home, entering the house, or picking up her mail, she stared at the sealed envelope in her hand.

Her hands shook as she peeled open the card.

Dear Carson,

I'm sorry about the other day. I can't explain why I had to lie. But enclosed is a wedding invitation. Please come and let's celebrate a new life and stop mourning past lives. I hope to see you there.

Teddy

Carson ran to her desk. She pulled open the door and grabbed the love letter to Emily from M.

"Oh my god, they match. Teddy is M." She had to call Hunter. She went to grab the phone and noticed the blinking answering machine for the first time.

A little spark of hope stirred in her chest. What if it were Hunter calling to say he didn't mean it? What if he wanted to give their relationship a shot? Would she take a chance on the man?

Yes, she would; and with that acknowledgement, a sudden burden left her heart. She wanted something with Hunter, and she no longer wanted to hide from it. Her finger pressed the button in anticipation.

The elation of expectation of hearing Hunter's voice turned to fear at the sound of Melinda's hurried voice.

"Carson, I didn't know what else to do. I don't know how much time I have. It's a matter of life and death. Please as soon as you get this message, meet me at the Starbucks in Franklin. It's six p.m."

Carson checked her watch. It was six thirty. She bolted out the door, hoping it wasn't too late to save Melinda's life.

Chapter 29

Carson spotted Melinda at a corner table near the window. Although her mane of red hair was tucked into a short blond wig, there was no disguising the long-legged beauty.

"Melinda." She jumped at the sound of her name, knocking her cup over. Lucky for the both of them, it was empty.

"I'm sorry, I didn't mean to frighten you."

"No. You're not the one frightening me. I'm sorry I've had to involve you in this." Her eyes darted around the room.

"Do you want to tell me what's going on?" Carson sat in the wooden seat across from her.

"Do you mind if I get another coffee first?" She rose from the table.

"Sure, go right ahead."

"Can I get you something?"

Carson pondered it for a second. She wasn't one to pass up a Starbucks coffee. "No, I'm good."

"Come on. It's my treat. It's the least I could do."

"Okay, that'd be great. I'll take a tall decaf, nonfat, toffee nut latte."

"Coming right up." She smiled.

Carson watched Melinda while she stood in the five-person line. Any one watching her would never know the woman was scared half out of her mind. She stood tall, composed, and confident. The only thing that gave her away was the constant turning of her head every time someone new came into the coffeehouse. Carson wished the line would speed up so she could get to the bottom of this strange new kinship she found herself in with this stranger.

"Gosh, this place is a goldmine." Melinda handed Carson her coffee. "Whoever thought there'd be a day that people would line up for a four-dollar cup of coffee."

Carson smiled as she took the cup. "I know what you mean." She took a sip. "Gosh, this stuff is awesome."

They both sipped their coffee in silence. Carson decided to wait for Melinda to make the first move. She didn't want to rush or scare her from her mission. She didn't have to wait too long before Melinda began to speak.

"I'm afraid of Teddy," she blurted.

Carson took in a deep breath. "Go on." She felt a deep-seated sadness. She knew that's what Melinda was going to say, but a huge part of her had hoped she'd be wrong. She wished Hunter was beside her. When she called to tell him about her discovery, his partner told her that he was out. She left an urgent message. She only hoped he'd believe her and get in touch.

"I-it's . . . god . . . I can't believe I'm doing this." Melinda's hand shook as she wrapped it around her coffee cup. "You have to know that I love Teddy more than life itself. I mean, he's my world. I—"

"Of course, you do. I don't doubt that." She patted her hand. "But you know as well as I do that we need to get him some help."

"What are you saying?"

"Melinda, we both know why I'm here. He killed Emily, didn't he?"

Carson watched Melinda's lower lip tremble as she caught it between her teeth.

"Yes." She nodded. "I believe he did, and I think I'm going to be next."

"Not if I can help it. Look, I know this wonderful detective. We'll just go down to his office, and you tell him everything you know."

"No, no police. I can't do that."

"Melinda, it's the only way. Do you want him to keep killing?"

"I don't have any proof. What, do I just walk in there and go 'I'm sorry, my fiancé's been acting a little weird lately, and I think that makes him a homicidal maniac.'"

"You don't need proof. I have it."

"What? What are you talking about?"

Carson opened her purse and pulled out both letters.

"Here." She handed them to Melinda.

"What is this?"

"Read them."

Carson sipped her coffee while she watched the tears slowly trickle down Melinda's ivory face.

Melinda looked up. "I don't understand."

"I found the love letter among Emily's things right after she died. She'd been home for a week, and no one knew about it. She was secretly meeting Teddy. I believe they'd been lovers for some time. I'm sorry."

"No, that isn't true. He loves me, doesn't he?" Her eyes pleaded with Carson to reassure her.

"I'm sure he loved you in his own sick way. But he's dangerous, and we need to bring this to the police."

"I don't know. I don't know if I can do it."

"Melinda, it's the only way."

"I need to think, to hide. Maybe I could stay with you for a couple of days just until I figure out what to do. I'll be safe with you."

"Melinda—"

"Please, Carson. I just need some time."

Carson had no other choice. She couldn't take the chance of Melinda disappearing and letting Teddy get away with murder. Carson knew Melinda would be safe at her house because Teddy would never link the two of them together. One day, two tops, that's how much time she'd give her; then they were going to Hunter.

"Okay, you can stay at my house. But only for a day or two, then we talk to Detective Reeves."

"You have a deal."

"Where's your car? You can follow me to my apartment."

"I don't have my car."

Carson stopped to stare at her. "How did you get here?"

"I left my car in downtown Nashville and took a taxi here. I was afraid he'd see my car and find me."

Carson contemplated Melinda for a moment. She was either pretty smart, or she watched too many spy movies and now lived paranoid. "That was good thinking."

"Whoa." Carson grabbed the edge of the table as she stood up.

"Are you okay?"

"Yeah, I think so. I felt a little dizzy. You didn't forget to make my coffee decaf, did you?"

"I told her that. Does it affect you that bad?"

"No, it's just I haven't had a real cup of coffee in seven years, and so it acts like a stimulant." Carson shook her head. "It could also be the fact that it's after seven, and I haven't eaten today."

"Do you want me to get you a muffin or something?"

"No, I'll be fine. I have food at the house, and it's only a few minutes from here."

They both walked out of the coffeehouse. Carson stopped to grab her stomach. Nausea swamped her. "Jeez." Maybe she finally got that stupid flu that was going around.

"Carson, what's wrong?" Melinda grabbed her arm.

"I think I have some flu bug. Would you mind driving?" Carson handed her the keys.

"No, just tell me where to go."

Carson mumbled directions as she curled up in the passenger seat. Her mind swirled as her stomach clenched into a million knots. Her last thoughts before she passed out was dying would be better than this.

Chapter 30

Cold, Carson felt so cold. And her head, it felt as though someone had taken an axe and whacked her in the middle of the skull. While her body ached all over from all the little needles she felt pricking her skin.

"Hey, sleeping beauty. It's time to get up."

The singsong voice buzzed in Carson's ear. She tried to swat it away, but her arm refused to move. What the hell was wrong with her?

"Go away." Was that froglike voice hers? She licked her parched lips. Her throat was on fire.

"Get up. You've been asleep long enough." The little lark voice became a sound of pure evil.

Carson willed her eyes to open, but they refused. Sleep, that's what she needed. Just a little more sleep. She pulled deep inside herself, trying to get back to the safe place. Then her body jerked to life as ice-cold water sluiced across her face.

She sputtered, rolled onto her stomach, and pulled herself up on hands and knees. She wretched.

"It's about time you got up." The evil voice returned.

Carson shook the water from her head. But the fuzzy haze lingered in her brain. Pulling up her head, she looked at Melinda.

"Melinda, what's going on? Where are we?"

"We're in hell."

Carson looked around. They were in the woods. The small clearing surrounded by little white candles.

"Oh god, Teddy found us, didn't he? Quick, help me up so when can get out of here." She reached out her hand.

Nothing happened.

"Melinda?"

A sudden breeze cut through Carson. She focused her eyes. Melinda towered above her, fully clothed, a look of pure malice etched across her face. Another rush of cold air covered Carson's body. She looked down to find herself clad in only a T-shirt and panties.

"Where are my clothes?" She shivered. "And where's Teddy?"

"God, you really are a double D bimbo, aren't you?" Her booted foot jammed into Carson's stomach.

"Humph." Carson curled into a ball. Then she screamed as her head jerked back.

Melinda came nose to nose with her. The beautiful redhead was replaced by an evil madwoman.

"What do you have to say for yourself?" Melinda slammed Carson's head onto the hard ground then released her death grip from Carson's hair.

Carson groaned and grabbed her throbbing head. How could she have been so stupid? She needed to fight through the pain and get away from the psychopath. Maybe if she kept her talking, she'd buy enough time to come up with a plan. That's how it worked on TV. Killers always wanted to talk about how smart they are.

"Why are you doing this?"

"Don't play innocent with me, you stupid whore."

Carson braced herself for the onslaught. Luckily, she only got a whiff of dirt and leaves kicked into her face.

"I swear, I don't know what I did." She tried to tamp down her fear as she got back to her hands and knees.

"You thought you could take him away from me. Just like Emily did." Melinda kicked more dirt.

Carson had almost made it to her feet but stumbled back against a tree on Melinda's last words.

"What?"

Melinda's ranting was replaced by a blood-curdling laugh.

"Yeah, she finally gets it." Melinda clapped her hands and danced in a circle.

"You know, she was much prettier than you, but then you do have a sexier body.

Carson crossed her arms over her thin T-shirt.

"Oh, please." Melinda rolled her eyes. I don't swing that way. Too bad for you that I don't. Because if I did, you wouldn't be in this predicament." She laughed, and the sinister sound echoed through the trees for what seemed eternity.

Carson made it to her feet but still couldn't focus enough to push away from the tree.

"Wow."

Carson froze.

"You're a lot stronger than she was. Emily never even made it off the ground."

"Why? Why me?" Carson mewled.

Melinda stared at her. Disgust marred her features.

"You really are stupid. I'd hope if Teddy were going to leave me for a tramp like you, you'd have some intelligence. But you truly are just a buxom bimbo with a talent in the bedroom. Why else would any decent guy want you?"

Carson wanted to knock her teeth in, but the more she thought she was stupid, the better chance she had of escaping. She just needed to keep her talking.

"I'm not sleeping with Teddy." She sounded pathetic.

"Huh. That's exactly what Emily said before I watched her drown."

She looked into Melinda's eyes. Not an ounce of remorse came from the wacko.

Fear swamped Carson as she looked into the face of this crazy woman. Hunter's warnings and fear tactics invaded her brain. Her childhood fears of monsters under her bed didn't even compare to this night. She was going to die for no reason, but then again, how many other innocents had died at the hands of psychopaths.

She shook the morbid, hazy thoughts from her mind. Now was not a good time to feel sorry for herself. She needed to keep Melinda talking.

"How could you kill an innocent person?"

"Innocent! Innocent! There was nothing innocent about the bitch. She was a dirty little whore who didn't deserve to live."

"She was a good, warm-hearted person. She and Teddy were soul mates. Bound together forever even before you came along. You should have accepted that and moved on."

"Right, soul mates. She loved him so much she dumped him right out of high school. And why would she do that?" She paced. "Let's think about it."

"I know why"—Melinda snapped her fingers—"because she wanted a man with a better body and a great job. And Teddy didn't become that until I made him that. He was nothing when I met him. He had a mediocre job, a so-so body, and his lovemaking skills were high-schoolish. But then I got him a job at my father's company. I got him into the gym, and I taught him how to make love to a woman. He thought he could take what I made him and give it to someone else. Never."

"So Teddy threatened to leave you, and you killed Emily." Her head started to become a little clearer.

"No, he's not leaving me. But I knew. I found his letters, and I followed him to Hawaii. And I watched as they spent three days playing lovers. I'd never give him the satisfaction of leaving me."

"No. You decided to commit murder instead."

"With her gone, he realized how much he truly loved me. And we set a date."

"So you have everything you want. Why kill me?" She balled her hands into fists.

"Everything was going good, then you showed up." She gritted her teeth. "He started to pull away again. I put two and two together and realized he replaced Emily with you. And now you have to die."

"You are so wrong. Teddy and I are only friends."

Carson still felt too weak. She needed to keep stalling.

"Liar!" She spat; then she took a deep-calming breath. "I've had enough. It's time."

"There is one thing I'm unsure of."

"And what's that?"

"I don't understand how you were able to get Emily to this place."

"That was quite easy. Ingenious, if I do say so myself." She smiled. "One little letter and like a dog in heat, she came running. You should have seen her face when I came out of the trees and not Teddy. Priceless. Hey, that would make a great commercial. One stamp, forty-two cents. Half a tank of gas, twenty dollars. A dead whore, priceless." She cackled.

"You wrote the letter."

Melinda's blood-curdling laugh ended abruptly. "Of course, Teddy's not that stupid?"

Carson swallowed. "Oh god, Teddy."

"Oh god, Teddy," she mimicked. "Some friend you are. Believing my sweet big teddy bear could kill someone in cold blood. Especially that stupid bitch Emily. God, the putz actually thought he was in love with the mouse."

"He did love her. I can't believe he actually thought he loved someone like you."

"Shut the hell up. He does love me."

"Right, that's why you wrote that letter and killed her."

"A letter that no one knows about, but me and you. I have to tell you, you threw me for a loop when you produced that letter. Emily and Teddy were being so careful. I was positive she would have gotten rid of it."

"You didn't know Em too well. She kept everything. So the gig is up." She watched Melinda contemplate the situation.

"That could be a problem." She tapped her fingers against her lips. "Oh, wait." She giggled. "I forgot. There is no more letter." She smiled.

Carson smiled back. This could be a way out. "That's where you're wrong. Detective Reeves has a copy of the letter."

"You're lying."

"Are you so sure?"

"You're not that smart."

"I'm a lot like Emily. You underestimated her." Carson shrugged.

"They don't know who it's from. So it doesn't matter."

"That's not true. We know who it's from."

"You're lying. You just said you didn't know I wrote the letter."

"No, I didn't know it was you, but it doesn't mean we didn't have someone else in mind."

"Duh, I'm still protected."

"Yeah, but Teddy's not."

"What?"

Now Carson smiled. "That's what the police think. And if I show up dead—" She shrugged. "Well, who's to say Teddy won't be the first person they go after. And all of your hard work would be for nothing because your precious Teddy will be behind bars for life."

"You're lying."

"Suit yourself. But if I were you, I wouldn't take such a chance. Especially after everything you've been through."

"Well, I guess we'll have to make sure you don't show up dead."

Carson felt only a slight bit of relief.

"I'll just make sure you don't surface."

Great, way to go, Carson. Now the psychopath will probably chop her up and dispense of her like Jimmy Hoffa. She needed more time.

"But, but how can you be so sure no one will find me. They found Emily."

"Of course they did. I wanted her to be found. I didn't want Teddy pining over her. Hoping she'd come back. This way, he knew she'd never be available."

The woman was sick. Carson wanted to throw up, but now was not the time to be weak. She needed to keep her talking. Carson managed to move away from the tree. "You'll never get away with it."

"I already have." Melinda pulled a bottle out of her coat.

Carson blinked at the bottle of tequila. She needed to think. There was no way she'd let her force that garbage down her throat.

"It won't work again."

"Of course, it will." She laughed.

"Still, what if someone happens to find me. That'd be pretty suspicious. Two women—best friends—dying in the same lake, and both by tequila. What are the chances? There will be an investigation. Can you take that chance?"

"Actually, I can. See, Teddy told me a lot about you and Emily. It seems you were always jealous of Emily. You wanted to be her so bad, have her life. So why not go out the same way she did. Would anyone be surprised? You have become obsessed by her death, alienated your friends, even that good-looking cop has given up on you."

Carson stared hard at her. "What did you say?"

"Honey, did you think I just thought about this today and planned it. I've been watching you for a while. I was there outside the house when he wiped his hands of you. And I have to say, it was pretty pathetic. I almost felt sorry for you. Until I realized if your cop friend dumped you"—she cocked her head to the side and smirked—"then you'd definitely try to stick your fangs into Teddy."

She tapped her finger to her chin. "Now that I think of it, it's too bad you couldn't keep the cop. It might have saved your life. Oh well, I doubt you're really going to be missed."

Carson let Melinda's words take hold of her. She was right. No one would miss her, especially Hunter. He had wiped his hands off her, and now he'd never know how she felt.

"Oh, poor little Carson, reality finally sets into her pea brain. No one's going to care if she lives or dies. Boo-freaking-hoo." Melinda's balled hands simulated a crying motion.

Melinda fell like a sack of potatoes as Carson barreled into her. The bottle flew out of Melinda's hand. Carson tried to punch her, but she spent all her energy tackling the psycho. She struggled to stay on top of her, but Melinda bucked her off like she was a seasoned rodeo rider.

"Nice try." Melinda got to her feet and brushed the dirt off her hands.

Carson lay sprawled on her back, willing her body to move. Within seconds, Melinda knelt over top of her. She pulled up Carson's head.

Carson clamped her lips shut while shaking her head side to side, forcing the tequila to splash across her face.

"You're going to make this hard, aren't you?" Melinda pinched Carson's nose closed.

Unable to hold her breath, Carson's mouth opened for a breath. She sputtered as tequila slid down her throat.

Chapter 31

Melinda released Carson as soon as she started to choke.

Carson rolled to her side, spitting out as much of the tequila as she could. It wasn't much. She wiped the spit from her mouth. The warm liquor burned a path to her stomach.

"We're not quite finished." Melinda flashed the half-empty tequila bottle into her face.

"I can't . . ."

"Noooo." The scream echoed through the clearing.

Melinda jumped and stared into the dark black woods. "What the hell was that?"

Carson used her elbows to push herself up and didn't get past that point. Her head lolled to the side as she, too, tried to pick something up in the darkness. The woods stood empty, and then a little blond head darted between the trees.

"What was that?" Melinda choked.

"Daniel," escaped from Carson's lips.

"What did you say?" Melinda got in Carson's face.

"I didn't say anything." Her head was too heavy for her shoulders.

Daniel raced through the trees again. His blond hair an eerie blur of white.

Carson's head began to swim. "Emily?"

"Emily? I guess the tequila's working. Because, honey, Emily is dead; and I don't believe in ghosts."

"Daniel, Emily, Dan—" Her elbows collapsed, sending her body crashing to the ground.

"Daniel." Melinda picked Carson's head up. "Who's Daniel?"

"Emmmeleee," Carson sung.

Daniel chose the moment to race between the trees again.

"That's it."

"Daniel, Daniel is it? My name's Melinda, and I am a friend of Carson's. You can come out now." She moved toward the trees.

The rustling stopped.

Carson fought the drunken state of her brain. She had to save him. She rolled to her side. Sweat trickled on her forehead as she tried to push up with her hand. She was only able to lift her head an inch from the ground in time to see Daniel inch his way out of the trees.

"Run, Daniel."

Melinda and Daniel both turned to her.

Daniel's eyes cut to hers. "Daniel, she's the water monster. Run and hide."

He looked back at Melinda then sprinted into the darkness.

"Shit." Melinda took after him.

Carson collapsed to the ground and breathed easier. She knew it was a good time to escape. But the tequila melted a warm path down her throat into her belly. The euphoria of not being cold made her giggle.

"What would Hunter do if he found me sprawled out half-naked like I am? Nothing," she barked into the cloudless sky.

She closed her eyes, letting sleep claim her.

"Car, Car, get up, please."

She swatted at the little fingers pressing into her flesh.

"Car, please don't go away," Daniel cried.

Carson's eyes popped open and looked into the face of an angel.

"Daniel." She shook her head to clear it. "Get out of here before she comes back.

"Not without you." He tugged at her arm.

"Daniel, listen. You don't understand." She peered into his frightened eyes. "I'm not strong enough. I need you to go to your house—"

"No one's there."

"Go to your neighbors' house and call 911 and get Detective Reeves."

"No, I'll take you to me and my dad's secret spot. The monster will never find us there. Just get up."

Desperate to get him to safety, she found herself getting to her feet. He pulled her hand. She made it three feet before swaying and falling to the ground.

"Daniel."

The sudden crackling of the brush echoed in the air.

"Oh god," Carson whined.

"Daniel, listen to me." She grabbed his little hand, giving him a squeeze. "Go to your hiding spot and stay there until the morning."

"Not without you. You have to come with me."

"Baby, I'll be okay. Trust me."

He refused to move.

"Hey, nothing's going to happen to me. I still owe you a ride in my convertible. You want to ride in it, don't you?"

He nodded. "But I can't leave you."

"Damn." She had to get him out of here. She made it to her knees. "You know that big guy that you've seen with me sometimes."

"Yes."

"Well, he's a cop, and he's on his way here to save me." She started as the crunch of shoes against leaves grew closer.

"The monster's back. Go."

He hugged her then took off into the trees.

"Well, it seems your little friend got away. But I'll find him—shit," Melinda screamed. "Okay, Carson. Come out. I know you're not strong enough. Just come out and face the music."

Carson bit down a yelp as her bare foot landed on a pine comb. She pushed back farther into the trees as Melinda's voice grew closer.

Her body shivered, and she felt the sheen of perspiration cover her body. The tequila wasn't mixing with whatever drug Melinda had given her. *Shake it off.* She only needed her body to hold it together just a few more minutes.

"All right, Carson. I've had enough. It's time to end this." Melinda moved into Carson's line of vision.

Come on, come on, come on, just a few more steps, Carson chanted in her head. Carson inhaled deeply as Melinda reached the spot Carson needed. With the half-empty tequila bottle in her hand, she charged

Melinda. She turned just as Carson smashed the bottle into Melinda's face.

"You bitch." Melinda looked down at her wet, bloodstained hand.

Before Carson could move, Melinda tackled her, sending them both into the lake.

The ice-cold water froze the blood in Carson's veins. She sputtered and spewed water when her head surfaced. Not that far from land, she tried to swim back, but a sudden yank of the hair stopped her.

"Oh, no you don't." Melinda grabbed a fistful of hair and began to swim away from the shore.

Carson ripped at Melinda's fingers, but to no avail. The tequila had finally finished her. Her noodle-limp arms fell to her sides, and she let Melinda pull her to the middle of the lake.

"Open your eyes." Melinda slapped Carson.

Her eyes popped open. Melinda got in her face, but she was nothing but a blur in Carson's eyes.

"Just wanted to say good-bye, bitch. Give your friend Emily my love, will ya?" She let her go and swam back to shore.

Carson watched her go. She willed her arms to swim, but she couldn't get them above the water. Then Melinda began to fade from her eyesight as she sank.

The cold began to leave. A sense of peace filled her. With a smile, she opened her eyes, and Emily stood in front of her.

"Emily. God, I've missed you." She reached out, but Emily moved away from her.

"Em?"

"No." Emily shook her head. Tears streamed down her face.

"I want to stay with you," Carson begged.

"You can't, you have to go now."

"I can't. I'm so tired. I just want the hurt to stop, and I want to forget. I want you back. Why couldn't you trust in our friendship and me? You wouldn't be dead now."

"I know and I'm sorry. I'll always be there."

"Don't leave. It's too late. I'll never make it back."

"I'll help you." Emily moved closer.

Carson reached for her, but suddenly something grabbed her around the waist, yanking her to the surface.

"Carson, Carson. Wake up. Don't die on me now."

She opened her eyes. The lake and clearing were bathed in light from the police helicopter. "Hunter. I—"

"Shhh." He lightly kissed her lips then tightened his hold on her as he began to swim to shore.

She clasped her arms around his neck before everything went black.

Chapter 32

Carson opened her eyes, and Melinda loomed over her, a pillow in her hand descending toward Carson's face. She tried to scream, but only a peep squeezed out of her raw-scratched throat. Her arms flailed as she tired to prevent Melinda from finishing her job.

Within seconds a, viselike grip pinned her arms to her side.

"Carson, wake up."

She stilled and then opened her eyes. Melinda turned into Hunter.

"Hunter." His name but a whisper from her lips.

"You're all right. It's over. You're going to be hoarse for a few days, but other than that, you're doing just fine."

"Mel—"

"Shh. Don't try to talk. Melinda's going away for a very long time."

"Teddy." *Gosh, it hurt to talk.* "How did you find me?"

"If it weren't for Teddy, you'd probably be dead right now."

She watched him and could have sworn she saw a shiver run through him. She continued to look at him, so he proceeded.

"Apparently, after you told him about your suspicions that Emily had been murdered, he began to suspect Melinda. She didn't do too good of a job covering her tracks. He discovered she had been to Hawaii when he had and when you told him about the letter. He didn't write it. He said he'd been trying to get a hold of you, but you didn't return his calls. Then when Melinda told him she was spending the night with a close girl friend, he got suspicious. And when he couldn't reach you, he got a hold of me. We didn't know how much of a head start Melinda had. When I reached the spot where Emily had been killed and didn't find you there," he paused, "then I ran into a little friend of yours, and he took me to you."

"Daniel?"

"He's fine, and he's been waiting to see you."

Hunter got up and opened the door. And her little blond knight in shining armor barreled through the door.

Carson smiled. "I told you I'd be okay."

He smiled back "So when can we ride in the convertible?"

Carson shut her suitcase. It had been two days since she woke up in the hospital. Her throat still burned a little, but the rest of her felt fine. And for the first time in a month, Emily no longer haunted Carson. She smiled as she remembered Emily saving her life. She decided to keep that bit of information all to herself. She doubted anyone would believe her. She was about to grab the suitcase off the bed when she heard a knock on the door.

"I'm ready—" She turned, expecting to see Hunter, but it wasn't him.

"Mrs. J."

"Hi, Carson. I wanted to come sooner, but I just . . . I couldn't . . . Carson, I'm so sorry for everything I said."

"It's okay, Mrs. J."

"No." She shook her head. "What I said was horrible, and I didn't mean any of it. I was just hurting. I miss her so much."

"I know. I do too." Carson dropped her suitcase and gave her a hug.

Mrs. J pulled away. "And all the guilt I felt for trying to force her into rehab. I kept thinking if I hadn't have done that, then maybe she'd still be alive today."

"Mrs. J, you had nothing to do with Emily's death." Carson hugged her again.

Mrs. J began to cry. "Then I heard what happened to you, and all I could think about was I couldn't stand it if I lost another daughter."

Carson froze then pulled away. "Mrs. J."

"You've always been like a daughter to me. I love you. I want to thank you for believing in Emily and finding her killer. If you ever put yourself in that kind of danger again, I'll kill you myself."

"I second that."

Both of them turned to look at Hunter.

"Neither of you have to worry. My PI days are over." Carson smiled.

"Detective, I want to thank you for saving Carson's life."

"It was my pleasure."

"Well, lets get you out of this hospital." Mrs. Johnson put her arm around Carson. Hunter followed with her suitcase.